GIFTED HEARTS

SHORT LOVE STORIES OF CARUM SOUND

BRANDI SPENCER

Authors 4 Authors Publishing

Marysville, WA, USA

©2021 Brandi Spencer
First published as *Idylls of Carum Sound* ©2019 B. C. Marine

"Seeing Through Him" ©2018 B. C. Marine.
First published in *Of Legend and Lore: A Collection of Fairy Tale Retellings.*
"Her Dearest Treasure" ©2016 B. C. Marine.
First published in *From the Stories of Old: A Collection of Fairy Tale Retellings.*
"I Loved You Tomorrow" ©2019 B. C. Marine.
"The Veiled Queen" ©2018 B. C. Marine.
First published in *A Bit of Magic: A Collection of Fairy Tale Retellings.*

Published by Authors 4 Authors Publishing
1214 6th St
Marysville, WA 98270
www.authors4authorspublishing.com

Library of Congress Control Number: 2021947819

E-book ISBN: 978-1-64477-129-7
Print ISBN: 978-1-64477-130-3

Cover and interior design by Brandi Spencer
Cover Photo ©2019 3rd Gen Photography. All rights reserved.

Author Photo courtesy of 3rd Gen Photography.

Authors 4 Authors branding is set in Bavire. Headings and titles are set in Athena. Correspondence is set in Almendra. All other text is set in Garamond.

GIFTED HEARTS

BRANDI SPENCER

Authors 4 Authors Content Rating

This title has been rated 14+ appropriate for teens and contains:

- moderate language
- brief implied sex
- moderate alcohol use

Please, keep the following in mind when using our rating system:

1. A content rating is not a measure of quality.

Great stories can be found for every audience. One book with many content warnings and another with none at all may be of equal depth and sophistication. Our ratings can work both ways: to avoid content or to find it.

2. Ratings are merely a tool.

For our young adult (YA) and children's titles, age ratings are generalized suggestions. For parents, our descriptive ratings can help you make informed decisions, but at the end of the day, only you know what kinds of content are appropriate for your individual child. This is why we provide details in addition to the general age rating.

For more information on our rating system, please, visit our Content Guide at: www.authors4authorspublishing.com/books/ratings

TABLE OF CONTENTS

WORKS BY BRANDI SPENCER

Healers' Kiss:

Kiss of Treason
Kiss of Destiny
Kiss of Legacy (July 2023)

Tied Tongues (September 2023)

Gifted Hearts:
Short Love Stories of Carum Sound

"Her Dearest Treasure"
"I Loved You Tomorrow"
"Seeing Through Him"
"The Veiled Queen"

SEEING THROUGH HIM

a retelling of *Beauty and the Beast*

With every pass of the polishing cloth, the glass cleared, revealing a curving river of dark auburn in the reflection. Rosabella leaned in, rubbing harder, willing the surface smooth. Ocean blue eyes floated lopsidedly in an uneven tawny face. She buffed one last section. With every movement, the distortion traveled around her head. Full but crooked lips tightened into a frown.

She groaned. "Warped again?" Tossing the cloth into a basket, she slumped into a chair.

Six months. For six months, Rosabella had apprenticed under Mistress Elba, master mirrorsmith, and her work was still worthless. At this rate, she would never become a master herself.

Her mentor set down her tools and crossed the forge to inspect the mirror. She gave a single curt nod of approval. "It's an improvement."

Rosabella scoffed. "You're just trying to make me feel better."

"No, really. The ripples are less pronounced than your last attempt."

"But it still doesn't show a true reflection."

Mistress Elba waved a hand. "You're too hard on yourself. Perfection requires time and patience."

Rosabella rubbed her temples. Her Allure could be a pain. No matter how many times she asked people to treat her normally, they couldn't help but be lenient with her. Being inherently likable made every compliment suspect and all too often softened or erased criticism. Mistress Elba was no exception.

Squinting, the master ran a hand over the mirror. "Most of the warping appears to be on the surface. The backing seems smooth enough...I can probably salvage this one." She bent down and inspected its profile. A few silvery strands escaped her thick ash brown braid. Her rugged fingers grazed the glass with a feather-light touch, liquefying the center.

A gentle smile crinkled the corners of her eyes as she straightened and dusted off her hands. "There. See, the defects were only superficial. Once it cools, you can frame it."

Rosabella crossed her arms over her thick leather apron. "But how would I fix it? I don't have Fire."

"I'll teach you the alternate method when you're ready."

"But—"

"You have enough to practice already," Mistress Elba said adamantly.

Rosabella sighed. "Maybe this was a mistake. My Gift is all wrong." It seemed as though all her lessons were the alternate ones.

Mistress Elba put a hand on her shoulder. "None of my former apprentices ever worked this hard."

None of them had needed to, but it would be rude to interrupt again.

"You've worn yourself ragged. Take a break. Go outside."

Of course, running errands. At least she could do that well. "Where do you need supplies from?"

"No, Rosabella, a real break, not a supply run. No more errands or practice or lessons today."

"It's barely past noon!"

Mistress Elba steered her toward the door. "I mean it. I need you to take a walk and clear your head."

"Mistress—"

She flung the door open and pointed. "Out!"

Rosabella snatched her poncho from a nearby hook and shuffled outside. "I'll be back in an hour," she grumbled over her shoulder.

Mistress Elba smiled and shook her head. "You're not coming back until dinnertime." She closed the door, leaving Rosabella standing agape outside.

Fine, then! If she wasn't needed... Rosabella took a deep calming breath. Compared to the stifling workshop, the warm, late spring air was refreshing. The street still glistened from the early morning rain. Townsfolk passed by, and Rosabella stepped aside to let a wealthy-looking couple into the shop. To her left, Pablo's bakery opened its windows, and the scent of fresh cornbread wafted out. Her stomach rumbled. Hours of hard but shoddy work had built up her appetite. She ducked inside and emerged a few minutes later with a sweet, golden treat.

But now what?

She knew all the shops here at the southern end of town, but she'd never visited the north side before. She'd never had half a day to kill, either, as she usually spent her rest days practicing. It was as good a time as any to explore the rest of Espejo.

After meandering for a few blocks, it became apparent why she'd never had reason to go there. Cedar cabins lined the road one after another, but shops were few and far between. Most were general stores, reselling merchandise from the market squares to those unwilling or unable to walk across town, all priced higher than at the original shops. One window even displayed a few of Mistress Elba's pieces alongside wares from all the top masters in town, from goldsmiths to tailors. Oh, to someday be the best in her own town. But for now, it was merely a dream.

Rosabella could have returned to the mirror shop, but Mistress Elba would have sent her back outside anyway. She wanted to trust in her master's judgment. After moving halfway across the kingdom to train under her, Rosabella couldn't return home unskilled. While few without Fire took up mirrorsmithing, Rosabella had been compelled to seek out Mistress Elba after seeing her work on display at a festival the year before. Copper spruce branches had surrounded a perfectly smooth glass oval. The blue-green patina that had formed over the frame only made the evergreens more lifelike. The shining surface held yet more beauty in its truthfulness.

If Rosabella could create something half as beautiful, she could open her own shop back home. But that wouldn't be enough for her. Having the wrong Gift for her profession meant working twice as hard and reaching twice as high. Yet here she was on a pointless walk when she could be practicing.

The farther she went, the more trees grew between the houses until the houses stopped entirely. She had passed into the forest now, and the sun filtered to the west through the evergreen canopy. Ferns and salal lined the path, weaving between the firs and cedars. Not far down the road, a wall of pink peeked out between pine trees. Curious, she picked up her pace and strode toward it.

Not a wall. Bushes.

Wild roses climbed ten feet high with clusters of blooms in all their five-petaled glory. Between them, a door opened into a cedar log cabin. Next door, smoke billowed out of a shed. Mistress Elba always told her to look for inspiration around her. Perhaps Rosabella could buy a rose cutting from whoever lived there. She poked her head through the cabin doorway but saw no one. She circled the outside and called, "Hello?"

Nobody answered.

Who would leave a smokehouse and an open cabin unattended in the woods? If a fire went wild, it could reach the town quickly.

As she circled the cabin again in search of a bucket of water, a momentary shimmer inside caught her eye, leading her inward. A simple log-frame bed covered in deerskin and a matching wooden nightstand stood at one end, with a river rock fireplace and oven at the other. A large pine table filled the center of the room with a single thick-spindled chair pulled up to its middle. Whoever lived there hadn't bothered to hang decorations anywhere. Next to the doorway, a small, plain wooden table held a silver hand mirror. Its intricately wrought details looked out of place in the otherwise sparse and rustic interior.

She picked up the mirror for a closer inspection. Ornate swirls and vines twisted up the handle and crept around its glossy face. Etching gave the effect of vines melting into the edge. Though she didn't recognize the handiwork, it was clearly a masterpiece.

"Hey!" a deep voice boomed. "What in the world are you doing?"

Rosabella started, dropping the hand mirror. No! It shattered on the floor. The sharp crack of glass pierced the air, breaking a piece of her soul with it. "I'm sorry. I didn't see anyone. I thought—" She turned around to face the speaker, but saw no one. She spun around completely, yet she still saw only an empty room.

The voice snickered. "Stop spinning. You're making me dizzy just looking at you."

She halted and backed toward the doorway. "I'm sorry about the mirror. I would never break such a piece on purpose, I swear."

"What are you doing here?"

She gripped the door frame behind her and looked around the small cabin. The velvet voice was definitely coming from inside and decidedly male. He sounded more annoyed than menacing, but that didn't help to loosen her fingers. "Please, show yourself first," she said in the most charming tone she could muster in her fear. "I'd like to converse in a more civilized manner." She stopped short of batting her eyelashes. Saving her own skin was one thing, but forcing Allure too much felt grimy.

He laughed. "I'm afraid you'll have to settle for uncivilized conversation." Slow, heavy footsteps echoed through the cabin. The chair moved across the room on its own, scraping across the rough wood floor. A deerskin pillow on the seat flattened, and the chair settled with a creak. "Now, what are you doing here?" he asked with less edge than before, letting his baritone warm into near sultriness. Forcing her Gift might have

4

been too much for him. No need to abuse her power—or give him any wrong ideas.

Rosabella had never met someone with Invisibility before. She let go of the door frame and took a step toward the chair, careful not to add to her natural Allure with a hip sway or sweet inflection. "I wanted to see if I could buy one of your beautiful roses; then I saw your smokehouse and thought your fire was unattended. Why did you wait so long to make yourself known?"

"Most people go away if I ignore them. They don't usually break my things."

"Again, I'm so sorry. I just wanted a closer look. I shouldn't have touched it." She picked up the frame by its handle and laid it on the entry table, then crouched down and began gingerly collecting the largest shards of glass. Such beautiful craftsmanship, destroyed. "I can get you a new mirror. With enough time, I might even be able to replace the glass in this one." She hated the thought of such a lovely frame being discarded.

He sighed. "It doesn't matter. It's just a mirror. I don't need it."

Rosabella raised an eyebrow in the general direction of the chair. "Just a mirror? It was a work of art. It would be a dishonor to my craft not to make it right."

"If it really bothers you that much..." The chair squeaked, and the cushion shifted and inflated. A leather bag vanished from the big table. The floorboards groaned. He was close enough now for her to faintly hear his steady breathing.

Holding her own breath, Rosabella looked for movement. What was he doing?

Shards disappeared from the floor one by one, followed by clinking sounds. With a louder clatter, the leather bag reappeared on the table next to the frame. Broken glass glittered inside. "You can put the pieces in here. There's a broom by the door for the rest."

Relieved, she hopped up and fetched the broom, and the chair creaked again. "You only have one chair?" she asked.

"What would I do with another one? I only have one butt."

Rosabella cleared her throat to mask a giggle. After making quick work of the mess, she wiped her hands on the work apron she'd forgotten to remove. "But what about when you have visitors?"

"I don't have visitors—and trespassers don't count."

How awful! How could anyone be completely alone? She couldn't fathom the idea. "No one at all? I—"

A far-off bell tolled, signaling the end of the day for shops in town.

"You should probably go back where you came from now," he said, disappointment overshadowing a tone of resignation.

This wouldn't do. Not when she could change it. Rosabella took the bag of broken glass and added the frame. She could use the pieces for mosaic work. "I'll return with a new mirror. I promise." She took two steps out the door before she popped back inside. "I never got your name—mine's Rosabella, by the way."

"Why do you care?" He sounded confused.

She shrugged. "I can call you 'Mister Not There' if you prefer."

He groaned. "No thank you. Call me Leandro."

"I look forward to seeing you again soon, Leandro," she said over her shoulder as she turned back outside.

"Ha. I won't hold my breath."

✿

Leandro tossed a branch from the roof, careful not to lose his footing in the process. It was finally dry enough to confidently venture onto the cedar shakes and remove the needles and branches that had accumulated, but the rains had still worn the wood smooth enough to give him pause. If he fell, nobody would come to his aid—they'd have to find him first.

It was a small price for his solitude. Why endure the noise and cramped spaces in town just to be unseen and ignored? People didn't interact with him either way, but at least here, he could have a little space to go along with the lack of conversation.

He swept pine needles off in fluttery green and brown clouds. Stray maple seeds followed, twirling over the roses and floating toward the path. In the distance, a tiny figure moved closer, weighed down by oddly-shaped cargo.

It couldn't be Rosabella. It had only been a few days, and she said it would take time to repair the glass.

Maybe she was visiting!

No. Why would she want to come back and visit a hopeless recluse? He sighed. Probably just a merchant.

Leandro finished sweeping, then dropped the broom in front of the door and inched over to the ladder on the back side of the house. By the time he reached the ground, someone was knocking on his door.

"Hello? Leandro?" Rosabella called out as he rounded the corner. She had tied a basket to the seat of a chair and used the extra rope for shoulder straps to carry it all on her back. The leather apron was gone, and her fitted lavender blouse flattered her more delicate features, though her strong arms still hinted at her trade. Dappled sunlight highlighted the red shimmer of her dark hair. She was downright stunning when she wasn't damaging his property.

"What are you—why—what is all this?" Such eloquence. Thankfully, she couldn't see the accompanying blush that warmed his cheeks. A simple greeting, and he melted like a fool.

"It's a rest day. The shops are closed." She grinned. "Want to see what I brought you?"

He tilted his head and opened the door. "I must admit I'm curious." More dumbfounded, really. Maybe he'd fallen off the roof and banged his head.

She reached out and patted the air with her hand before entering the cabin. In a few moments, she had the basket open on the kitchen table, and the smell of warm bread filled the room.

His mouth watered. Hunting and gathering had sustained him for years. The last time he'd had fresh goods from town was almost fifteen years ago, for his birthday. A strawberry- and cranberry-stuffed pastry. The morning of the Gifting ceremony, he couldn't wait for anything. He inhaled his breakfast and ran to the lodge. Had he known what would happen that day, he would've run away from it.

Not that it would've done any good. Invisibility would have found him anyway, but fear and logic rarely get along. Inducing his Gift at the ceremony should have made it easier to control. As he still had no idea how to turn it off, Leandro didn't want to imagine what even less control would be like. Mentors for rare Gifts were hard to come by, and in his case, impossible to find.

Unable to catch a clerk's attention in a busy bakery and unwilling to risk being mistaken for a thief, Leandro had given up on buying fresh bread, and most other goods in town for that matter. He didn't realize just how much he missed it until now.

Rosabella served a portion of bread and raspberries in front of his chair, then sat in the one she had brought and served herself. "I ran out of room for meat in the basket. I hope that's okay."

"I have some in the smokehouse," he said without thinking and made his way there. What was he doing, offering up his food? Just a few days ago, she was a trespassing vandal. But she drew him in, *alluring* him... Oh no. Could he be more oblivious? It was only the name of a stinking Gift. She had to be conning him using Allure. But why? She'd already broken the only thing of value he had. Torn between suspicion and attraction, he returned to the table with a piece of venison.

She reached into the basket, radiant with excitement—or perhaps it was part of her Allure—and pulled out the leather bag she had taken from the house before. She offered it to his chair. "I'm still working on your other one. This one's nowhere near as fine, but I didn't want to make you wait."

Leandro sat and took the bag. The mirror inside had a smooth wooden frame and handle, and the glass bowed slightly. Most likely a reject from the shop.

"I made it yesterday," she said, sitting up straighter. "Mistress Elba told me I could bring it to you, and you can keep it even after the other one is repaired."

He grimaced. Poor quality or not, he couldn't bring himself to insult the mirror when she seemed so proud of it. "Thank you. That's very...generous." He picked up the bread while it was still warm and dug in. Knowing she couldn't see, he ate with abandon, savoring every bite. He'd forgotten bread could be so sweet and savory at the same time.

Rosabella ate in peaceful silence herself for a few moments. Then began the telltale wriggling in her seat of someone uncomfortable with silence. Whatever she wanted, he wouldn't be the one to speak first. Let her squirm all she wanted.

"If it's not too rude to ask..." she said finally.

As if that had stopped her yet.

"What do you need a mirror for without a reflection?" She leaned forward. "Was it an heirloom?"

Should he answer? It seemed like a harmless enough question, but he still wasn't sure what she was playing at.

"I'm prying, aren't I? Was that too personal?"

"No, no. I've just never been asked before." Meh, why not? This particular knowledge couldn't do any harm. He plucked another two pieces from the basket and held one just above her plate. "You're right. I don't usually have a reflection. But I'm sure you've noticed that when I carry something or wear it, it turns invisible like me." He dropped the bread onto their plates, enjoying seeing her eyes widen at the sudden reappearance. "The hand mirror acts as part of me."

"Does that mean you're not invisible to yourself?"

He laughed. "Thank the Giver, no. It's bad enough that nobody else can see me." He shuddered. "Speaking of nosy questions..."

Rosabella raised an eyebrow.

"Why would someone like you work with her hands?"

"Someone like me?" she lied flimsily.

"You know, someone with your Gift." If he was wrong about the pull he felt and mentioned it aloud, she'd think he was flirting. Better to keep it vague.

She picked at the bread on her plate and said softly, "You noticed that."

"What can I say? I've become adept at observation. It comes with the territory."

Rosabella shrugged. "I need to do something, don't I? And I've always been drawn to mirrors."

"Wouldn't it be easier to use your Allure? You could marry rich or become a popular merchant easily. Why physically work?"

"Do *you* want to be defined by *your* Gift?" she asked, almost flirtatious in her confidence.

"We are. Whether we want to be is irrelevant."

She shook her head. "I refuse to accept that."

Maybe she wasn't a con artist after all. Just deluded.

Rosabella wiped her forehead as more droplets snuck down the back of her neck. The forest wasn't as sweltering as the town, but she still longed for the cool shade of Leandro's cabin. The weekly visits had become a welcome respite, especially as the summer heat hit its peak. After Rosabella returned that first evening with a renewed sense of purpose, Mistress Elba had encouraged her to continue to leave on rest days, telling Rosabella that more time spent away from the forge made her a better apprentice.

She smiled as the rosebushes came into sight. Their first blooms long gone, the thorny branches stood sentry over the tiny hideaway.

"Oh, good. You're here," Leandro called out before she had reached the doorway. "I need your help with something."

"Should I be worried?" He never asked for help; he barely tolerated visits. Even when she actively tried to be charming, he remained walled off.

"How adept are you with a pair of scissors?"

Ten minutes later, Rosabella stood behind Leandro's chair, a comb in one hand and shears in the other. "How did you talk me into this? What if I cut your ear off?"

"I'm watching in the mirror. I'll tell you if you get too close."

Sculpting red-hot glass and metal felt less dangerous than this, but she needed to fulfill the trust he'd placed in her, or she'd likely never see it again. She took a deep breath and slowly reached forward with the comb until her hand stopped.

"That would be my neck."

"Oh no!" She sprang her hands up in surrender. "I can't—I have no idea what I'm doing."

"Rosabella, it's fine. Put the comb in your other hand and hold it out for me."

She did as he asked, and a calloused hand wrapped around her wrist. He guided her up and forward, burying her fingers in dense, long hair. It was surprisingly soft and clean. As she ruffled the roots, hints of mint and pine implied a fresh washing, and she resisted the urge to lean closer and inhale the manly scent.

"That's the top of my head." He pulled her hand farther to the hairline, traveling down to his left ear. With a bit more force, he led her a few steps around to the side of the chair and moved her hand back to the apex. "You can start there." As he slid his hand away, he gave her fingers a slight, reassuring squeeze.

For a moment, the air under her hands pulsed in a hazy man-like shape, as faint as a shadow in the corner of one's eye, then disappeared. Rosabella blinked, but the image didn't return. She had seen only what she wanted to see.

After another calming breath, she combed out what felt like an even strip of hair and held it between her fingers. "This is probably going to look silly."

"What do I care? I'm not cavorting through town. As long as it feels cooler and lighter, it'll do."

"All right then." She snipped the shears just above her fingers. Eight inches of wavy maple brown hair flashed into view on its way down to the floor. She moved to his left and cut again. To the left once more—

"Wait. A little to the right."

She followed his directions. They carried on thusly until the right half of his head felt sufficiently shorn.

"How did you do this alone?" she asked, continuing to cut.

"I gathered it all at the base of my neck and cut that. It wasn't very effective."

"I can see that. I don't know if you're aware, but there are people in town who can do this professionally. We call them barbers."

"Very funny. You know I don't like people."

He was bluffing, but she played along, putting a hand on her hip. "I'm a person."

"You're different."

Rosabella scoffed.

Leandro grunted. "That's not what I meant. Allure has nothing to do with it. You're my only visitor. That's all. My own family hasn't even been here."

"Why not? Did you have a falling out?"

"Nothing so dramatic. I was often overlooked as a child, and when they couldn't see me anymore, it didn't take them long to forget me. After a couple of years, they forgot me for a week solid, and I just left."

At a loss for words, she rested a hand where she guessed his shoulder to be, and his hand enveloped hers for a moment.

He cleared his throat. "We should finish up soon. I'm hungry, and I'll have to sweep all this hair up before we can set the table."

Smiling internally, she nodded. For a moment, she'd glimpsed the man inside.

❁

Rosabella passed her latest work to Mistress Elba for inspection. It was a small piece, but the quality was high; she knew it. Nevertheless, Rosabella always dreaded the flaws her mentor would inevitably find.

"Beautiful repair, Rosabella. If I didn't know better, I'd say it looks new."

She nearly burst with delight. "Thank you, Mistress! I needed to get this one right."

Mistress Elba chuckled. "I'm not surprised. I know how important it was to you." With a wink, she handed back the elegant hand mirror. "I'm guessing you'd like to deliver it tomorrow?"

"My perfectionism has kept Leandro waiting long enough. I hope he's pleased with it."

"He will be. You've come a long way. In fact..." She picked up a drawing from the table. "I saw the design you've been sketching. I think you're ready to create it. There's a festival at the beginning of next month.

Mirrorsmiths from all over the kingdom will be here, competing for honors. I want you to enter the apprentice contest."

"You think I can complete it in time?" Rosabella asked. "I've never tried something that complex."

"I'll lighten your list of chores."

"But what about getting your orders done on time?"

Mistress Elba waved the comment away. "I managed just fine before you. I can handle a little less help for a short while. But, you need to do one thing for me."

Rosabella nodded. "Anything."

Mistress Elba put her hands on Rosabella's shoulders. "Make me proud."

❀

Leandro fiddled with the red leather ribbon in his hands. He'd dyed the deer hide himself. Invisibility made hunting easier, and he had no shortage of meat and pelts. A cloth ribbon would've been more traditional, but the spirit of the gesture demanded frugality, so leather it was.

He checked out the window. Still no sign of Rosabella, although she wasn't due for another twenty minutes.

He loosened his grip on the ribbon. If he tore it apart before she arrived, it wouldn't be much use. Such a small token—which was entirely the point—but to him, it meant everything. The ribbon of intent. If she accepted the offering, he could woo her openly, as propriety dictated. And if that went well...

Maybe she was right about not being defined by Gifts. Maybe they could have more.

He just had to get this part right first. When he'd left town, he'd been just old enough to know the basic requirements, but young enough to never have tried them. Hopefully, neither his memory nor passing fashions had altered what little he knew.

Footsteps outside broke his reverie. Rosabella bounded through the door, holding a small package aloft and dazzling him with her smile. "Look what I have!" She set it gingerly on the entry table.

"Is that what I think it is?"

"Take a look. I did the work myself."

He unwrapped the coarse ramie cloth to reveal familiar silver. His old mirror, just as he remembered it. He picked it up to see his scruffy reflection smiling back at him. Maybe it was for the best that she couldn't

12

see his unkempt appearance. At least he bathed regularly. Unwashed man-stink scared away game.

"Do you like it?" she asked, inching closer.

"It's perfect." Could he do this? It was just a ribbon, not a ring. But now that she was here, his resolve faltered.

"Good. Speaking of mirrors, there's a festival in a few weeks..." She traced the wood grain on the table with her finger.

"The Festival of Reflection?"

Her head popped up. "You know about it? I thought you didn't go into town."

"Well, I was born there."

"Fair enough. Anyway, I'm working on a piece to enter." She fidgeted again, moving her hands to the back of the chair she would normally have sat in by now.

"I hope you can bring it by. I'd love to see it." It was more than flattery. The improvement between the first mirror she'd brought him and this one was impressive.

"It'll be too large to just bring out here, I'm afraid."

"Oh. That's too bad. You'll have to tell me how it fares, at least."

She smiled sweetly. "Why don't you come with me? We could have so much fun. I hear there's even dancing in the evening."

"No. I can't." The thoughtless words came of their own accord.

Rosabella frowned. "But—"

"I don't dance. I don't go into town."

"I know. You hate getting lost in the crowd, but I'll be right by your side."

What had he been thinking? He couldn't court her. He couldn't court anyone. That might lead to marriage. Then he'd have to go into town, maybe even live there. And she couldn't live out here in the woods without a forge and a shop, not when the market was on the opposite edge of town. She only visited once a week; she wouldn't want to make that trek every day. He crushed the ribbon in his hand and closed his eyes, wishing away his foolish dream. Why had he let her in? Her presence only fueled desires that could never be filled.

"Leandro, please. Just talk to me." She reached out to him, just shy of his location, grasping empty air.

"There's nothing to talk about." He said it more harshly than he intended.

"Why are you so upset?"

"You're demanding too much of me."

"Demanding?" She rolled her eyes. "It's just an invitation. You're overreacting."

"Why are you even here?"

She tilted her head. "What is that supposed to mean?"

"Why are you here?" he enunciated.

Rosabella crossed her arms. "I'm returning your mirror, and I *thought* we could have a pleasant lunch together."

"No. Why are you here? Why do you keep coming back? What are you getting out of all this?"

She shrugged. "I wanted to be your friend."

"You have no trouble making friends. You probably have more than you know what to do with."

"So what? Yes, I *can* make friends easily. But believe it or not, I choose to do so with people I *want* to be friends with."

"Why me?"

"Because you needed one."

As if he didn't already feel like dirt. "I don't need your pity," he spat.

Her eyes widened. "It's not—"

"You might as well leave." Each word he spoke tore at him, but it had to be done.

"Leandro!" She reached forward with more force, stumbling when he stepped deftly out of the way. Steadying herself on the table, she scanned the room for signs of him, though he did not move.

"You aren't obligated to keep returning here—"

"Please, don't do this—"

"And I don't want you to."

Her shining blue eyes allied with his heart, pleading for him to stop. If he didn't do this now and let things progress instead, it would only hurt worse when everything inevitably fell apart. He opened the door.

She walked through and stopped just outside, turning back to say, "Don't shut me out, Leandro. You don't have to be alone."

He forced himself to say, "Goodbye, Rosabella," and closed the door.

He marched to the fireplace, wadding up the ribbon, prepared to hurl it in, but his arm would not cooperate. The trinket was worthless to him now, and yet he couldn't bring himself to destroy it. No more destruction. Not in that moment. He let go.

As the ribbon fell to the floor, Leandro dropped into his chair, head in his hands, and wept.

14

Rosabella was wrong. He would be alone forever.

❁

The copper strip snapped in two as Rosabella stretched it. "Frog nuggets!" She slammed the pieces on the table.

"Gently this time," Mistress Elba said. "Again."

Rosabella heated and quenched another piece and pulled again, determined to be gentle, but her tense fingers did not obey. It, too, broke under the strain.

Pressure built up inside her chest, spreading into clenched hands and clouding her vision. She closed her eyes. The moisture that escaped between her lashes stung in the dry heat.

Mistress Elba's tools clanked against the table, and a hand squeezed her shoulder. "Let it out," the master said.

Rosabella wiped her cheek with the back of her wrist. "Curse my hands. I'm just so clumsy today."

"That's not it. You've been in a mood for days."

Rosabella put a hand up. "It's personal."

"It affects your work in my shop. That's not personal anymore."

Rosabella's breath hitched. "I'll keep it to myself better."

"No. Trying to hide your pain is the problem. What we do is art. Don't fight the pain. *Use it.*"

She looked at her mentor, confused. "Use it?"

"Follow me." Mistress Elba led the way into the gallery. "Look at these." She pointed to a shelf of poor but salable mirrors that Rosabella had made months ago. "When you started, you were so bent on perfection, you could never attain it. Now these." She pointed to a shelf of gleaming glass, simple but smooth. "When you stopped forcing it—when you embraced life—your work flourished."

Rosabella sighed. "Being happy made inspiration easy." Couldn't Mistress Elba leave well enough alone? Why turn the knife?

"Yes, you channeled that happiness into beauty, but life isn't always happy. You must work with what you have. Feel your pain. Quench your scrollwork with your tears. Etch the glass with heartache. Use it. Put it on display."

"For everyone to see?" Rosabella recoiled.

"Our mirrors reflect their makers as much as their owners. If you cannot handle that, you've chosen the wrong profession." Mistress Elba's blunt tone held no contempt.

The spruce-framed mirror shone from the middle of the room, the same one that had inspired her before. "That piece is about renewal," Rosabella said instinctively.

"It was the first piece I made when I moved here, years ago. Never had the heart to sell it."

Rosabella looked at her own hands. What wonders could they produce? She walked back to the forge and took another piece of copper. As the metal warmed, she opened her heart, the raw emotion rising with the steam as she plunged the piece into water. She exhaled. Tears fell down her cheeks as she stretched the copper into a pointed leaf.

❁

Mistress Elba smiled. "If you don't win a prize tomorrow, I'll be shocked."

Rosabella feigned a smile in return. "Thank you, Mistress." The clear glass gleamed in its delicately sculpted frame. She rubbed the smooth metal foliage between her fingertips. As pleased as she was with how her mirror had turned out, something was missing—or rather, someone.

She knew Leandro had hurt himself with his outburst. Lack of practice made him a terrible liar. Why did he have to be so stubborn?

She would have traded all her best work to have him back. Even now, she fought the urge to run into the forest. If she poured on the charm as thick as honey, she might be able to persuade him to change his mind. But what good would that do? Affection meant nothing if it was coerced.

Maybe, given a little space and time to think, he'd let her back in. And maybe he was right about her demanding too much. Though she'd never said it aloud, part of her had wanted more; maybe he knew it. For now, she would try to enjoy the festival, even if it felt like dancing with a broken leg.

❁

Leandro stared at the ceiling. It was past time to get out of bed, but he had nothing to do. In an effort to keep the emptiness at bay, he'd thrown himself into scrubbing down every inch of the cabin. He'd chopped firewood. He'd weeded his garden. He'd done every chore he could think of, pausing only to collapse in bed each night. Even his meals were eaten while working.

There were no chores left, and he was alone. For the last eight years, he'd resigned himself to that fact, but after knowing Rosabella, Leandro finally knew what he was missing. He could no longer stave off the pain.

16

He flopped over and lurched to his feet. Shuffling across the room, he yawned and stretched his arms. Although he wasn't hungry, he willed himself to look in the pantry. He took a basket of blackberries and plopped them onto the table, then slumped into his chair. If he left the fruit to rot, he'd kick himself for it later.

He forced down a few handfuls, letting his vision blur out of focus with his thoughts. A rogue blackberry tumbled out of his grasp. It rolled across the table and fell onto Rosabella's empty chair.

What use was an extra chair? It needed to go.

Grabbing the chair by its back, he dragged it away. As he opened the door and swung the chair around it, he knocked the entry table. The silver hand mirror fell. Leandro dove, catching it at the last second. He groaned and rolled onto his side. Hardwood was not forgiving.

A glint caught the corner of his eye. His clumsiness had dislodged a piece of broken mirror from between the table and the wall. He reached out for the shard, part of his beard popping in view on its surface as he took hold.

Leandro squeezed his eyes shut. No! Must everything conspire to remind him of her today? Even now, the far-off voices of late travelers heading for the Festival of Reflection assaulted him. He hurled the shard outside, where it burst on a tree trunk.

Enough foolishness.

After a minute, he picked himself up off the floor. Leaving the mirror out on the table was stupid. He'd nearly broken it again. Besides, if he stashed it away, it couldn't taunt him all the time. He opened the drawer and shoved the mirror inside. But as he went to close it, a tangle of red stopped him cold. The ribbon of intent curled around his fingers as he cradled it in his palm.

If the Giver himself had condemned his folly aloud, he couldn't have felt it more keenly. He'd hoped to spare himself future pain, but nothing could be worse than this.

Before he could second-guess himself, he stepped outside and locked the door. Around him, the cluster roses paraded their second blooms. He stuffed the ribbon in his pocket. If he was going to go far enough to remedy his mistake, he might as well aim high.

✿

Leandro hung back against the outer wall of a shop at the edge of the market district. Just a few yards away, crowds of festival-goers filled the streets. On the emptier roads, he could walk far enough away from people to avoid interaction, letting thoughts of Rosabella distract him and urge him forward. But here, he would have to rub shoulders with others to pass by.

He shook out his nerves and bounced on the balls of his feet. It was too late; he couldn't return home—not after coming this far.

A quick inhale, and he dove into the crowd. Dodging elbows and weaving between revelers, he surged forward, into the heart of the festival. Tinsel and glass baubles hung overhead, strung on lines between buildings. As the name suggested, the mirrors were featured at the center of the Festival of Reflection. That's where he would find his own heart as well, if the crowds didn't suffocate him first. Unaware of his presence, person after person ran straight into him, causing ripples of minor, temporary panic in the crowd as the unseen obstacle startled them. Leandro did his best to jump out of their paths, but that often meant backing into someone else. Despite his great endurance, the sheer number of people wore him down as he progressed.

When he thought he could go no farther, the displays came into view. Behind ropes, various tables and stands held up dozens of mirrors, large and small, reflecting everyone and everything but him.

He knew the piece he was looking for instantly.

Wild roses surrounded a two-foot by three-foot rectangular mirror. Some were etched in the glass itself, and others had been formed in metal and cured into the perfect shade of pink. From a distance, it looked like a mirror nestled inside one of his real rosebushes.

He approached the piece, confident that he could still back away unnoticed if he didn't speak up. A small card tucked in the corner read, "Apprentice: Rosabella under Mistress Elba of Espejo."

A group of five judges were walking behind the ropes, stopping to inspect the mirrors and marking their cards as they went. Leandro waited until they passed nearby to venture closer for a peek. At least three had marked Rosabella for first in the apprentice class.

Her work had progressed so much. What if he was a distraction? She might be glad to be rid of him.

Behind him, Rosabella's laugh cut through the din. He turned. She sat at a table near the middle of the plaza, smiling and sharing lunch with two men: one young, the other much older. Both were enraptured by her, especially the doe-eyed younger man.

Leandro backed into the rope and sighed. She didn't need him. She could move on just fine. If he left now, she could forget him like everyone else, if she hadn't already.

✿

Rosabella nodded politely as Juan regaled her with his triumphs in the forge.

"...lifted the whole sheet myself," he said, flexing his bicep and winking.

It took all her strength to suppress an eye roll. Time to change the subject before that strength wore out. "Master Roberto, you've been awfully quiet."

"You know, I remember my first Festival of Reflection..."

Any other time, she would have eagerly picked the master's brain, but her own mind insisted on drifting away. Where was Mistress Elba? She should've been back from the shop minutes ago. Rosabella began to suspect she'd left her with them on purpose, the way she'd scurried off right after introductions. Why couldn't Mistress Elba keep her nose out of Rosabella's affairs? She didn't need her help; she could find someone new herself if she wanted to.

Rosabella scanned the crowd. Near their mirrors, the rope barricade pulled inward on its own and swayed. Hope welled up.

Leandro?

She watched the area for a few moments, waiting for another odd movement. Nothing. Of course not. She picked at her bread. It could have been the wind. She shouldn't let herself get excited so easily.

"Are you all right?" Master Roberto asked.

"It's nothing. I just thought I recognized someone." She glanced back at the rope.

"Maybe you did," a familiar voice rumbled.

A wild rose materialized in front of her. Around its stem, a crimson leather ribbon formed a tidy bow. She had rejected many ribbons of intent before, but this red one, wrinkled and mismatched with the pink flower, was the loveliest she'd ever seen.

"Leandro?" Rosabella covered her grin with both hands.

"You were right," he said. "I don't want to be alone. Not without you."

She picked up the rose and breathed in its sweet perfume. The ribbon untied easily. "It's beautiful." She tucked the bloom behind her ear.

Juan wrinkled his nose and arched an eyebrow to Master Roberto, who shook his head. Poor Leandro. His public declaration was sweet. He probably wasn't aware of his faux pas and certainly didn't deserve to be mocked for it.

"Excuse us," she said to the fellow smiths and held out a hand to Leandro.

He helped her off the bench and looped her arm through his. "Did I offend your admirers?" he whispered.

She chuckled. "Master Roberto is an old colleague of Mistress Elba, and his apprentice is competing with me."

"They didn't look happy."

"I think they were a little scandalized." She lowered her voice. "Some say it's coercive to offer in public; it doesn't let a woman decline gracefully."

He jerked to a stop. "I'm sorry."

"Don't be. I don't care what they think." She held up the ribbon and wrapped it around her wrist. "And don't believe for a second that I'm giving this back."

He tied off the ends then circled his arms around her. "If you don't care what people think, we could join the dancing later and look completely foolish."

Rosabella put a hand on his chest. "That sounds wonderful."

Beneath her hand, a rough gray tunic appeared, followed by tawny leather leggings and boots. His body blossomed into view, the maple brown hair and beard bringing out the gold flecks in his icy blue eyes. She thought no sight could ever fill her with more joy; then he caressed her cheek and leaned in closer, proving her wrong. Sliding her hands behind his neck, she closed the distance. His lips against hers tasted like bliss.

As she pulled away, she saw her mirror reflecting their embrace, revealing them both in perfect clarity. With a grin, Rosabella looked into Leandro's eyes and said, "I can see you."

HER DEAREST TREASURE

a retelling of "The Peasant's Clever Daughter"

The sun rarely shone on the soggy island of Baythroas, but that day, it warmed the golden cedar planks of the throne room. The polished walls washed everything inside with a faint tawny glow. Basil ran his hand along the arm of his throne, soaking up the heat from the wood, feeling it deep in his bones. He thought the day could not be any brighter. Then she walked in.

Accompanied by an older man, a young woman curtsied before him, wearing a rough dress the color of mud. Warm brown tendrils curled out of the braid falling down her shoulder and framed her bronze face. Objectively speaking, she was plain. Neither ugly nor pretty, nothing about her features should have made her stand out in a crowd. Indeed, the man, who appeared to be her father, was instantly forgettable. But she carried herself with a confident sense of purpose that caught Basil's attention.

"Your Majesty," she said, her dark amber eyes meeting his gaze, "my name is Sonia. My father George and I appeal to your kindness and humbly ask for your assistance."

He waved her on with a relaxed smile. "What is your request?"

"We have little more to our names than a two-room cabin just outside the village. We only survived this past winter with the help of our neighbors. I do not want to burden them again."

She did not mope or wring her hands as he had seen others with similar plights do. She stated the facts with her head held high. Only her eyes betrayed her emotions, eyes that had seen things he would never experience.

Basil crossed his arms. "So you wish to bring your burden to me instead?"

"Not exactly," she said with a hint of a laugh in her voice and a smile. "I believe we could be of benefit to you. My father is a good farmer, but we have no land to work. You have unused land next to our home. If you allowed us to cultivate it and increase your own stores, I thought we could keep a portion of the crops for ourselves."

He nodded. Between the lovely weather and the beguiling woman, he was feeling especially magnanimous. "I don't see the harm in your plan, provided you remember whose land you are using." He held his chin and tapped his lips with his forefinger, then said, "You may keep half the crops. That should leave you more than enough to not only eat but to sell. Everything else belongs to me."

She beamed and bowed deeply, her father mimicking her. "Thank you, Your Majesty. I'm sure your generosity will be rewarded this harvest."

A fine mist soaked Sonia's face and beaded on her hooded poncho as she covered the row of kernels with soil. She stopped for a moment, slamming her hoe into the edge of the field. The tiny log cabin nestled between the trees called out to her, but time was running out for planting. She sighed and picked up a bag of corn. Her father had been gone for three days now, leaving her to work alone. "Stupid earring...I told him not to go," she muttered.

She had found the golden earring when they were tilling. A sapphire, the size of her thumbnail, sat in the middle of it, surrounded by gold filigree. Her father had jumped with excitement. "The detail work is amazing," he said, examining it with his Near-Sight. "If only you could see all of it. This must be worth a fortune."

Sonia shrugged. Without the same Gift or a magnifying glass, she'd have to take his word for it about the craftsmanship, but the materials alone would fetch a good price.

"We should give it to the king," he had said. "It would only be right."

"I don't think that's a good idea."

"He was generous enough to let us use this field. It's the least we can do to thank him. Besides, by all rights, it belongs to him."

"But we only have one earring," Sonia said. "The king will want the whole pair. We should hold onto it until we find its mate. If you take it to him now, he'll think you're claiming half of it and cheating him."

Her father had brushed off her concerns. What did she know? It had only been her idea to ask the king for the land in the first place. The next morning, both he and the earring were gone, and she had not seen either since.

Sonia dropped the bag and picked up the hoe again.

A figure blurred by on the right, and a man dressed in a yellow uniform appeared on the edge of the field. He fidgeted impatiently as she trudged out to meet him. She suppressed a touch of envy. If she had Speed, she could have finished the field days ago.

"Are you Sonia?" he asked.

She nodded.

"I have a summons for you from King Basil." He handed her a small envelope with the Baythroan seal. She thanked the messenger, and in another blur, he sped away on foot, disappearing through the trees in a matter of moments.

She opened the letter, but it told her nothing specific, just that the king himself requested her presence. The summons had to be about her father. Part of her cursed him for ignoring her and getting himself into trouble, but another part was giddy with anticipation. She remembered the way the king had looked at her the last time, with a measure of respect she didn't often see. And she had to admit, King Basil wasn't too hard on the eyes either. She tried to clear the silly thought from her mind as she headed inside to clean up.

After stowing away the tools, she scrubbed herself down with pine soap and changed into her other dress. The short green garment was made of the same rough cloth as the brown one she had been working in, but at least it was clean and dry. Sonia wiped the worst of the mud from her poncho and tall boots.

As she left for the palace, she decided to look on the bright side. Even if she were right about the summons, it was still an opportunity to see the king. How many more of those would she get in her humble life?

♕

Sonia curtsied as a servant announced her. The king leaned forward, and an amused smile played at the corners of his mouth, highlighting his warm eyes and strong jaw. And were those dimples she saw? Her insides fluttered, though whether the cause was his royal status or his handsome features, she couldn't be sure.

With a deep, strong voice he said, "Your father has been in jail the last few days for withholding property. Every day, he has moaned to the guards that he should have listened to you. When I brought him back before me today, he said that you advised him not to bring the earring without its mate. I want to know: are you as clever as he claims? Did you really predict that I would think he kept its mate for himself?"

Sonia had no response to give. She couldn't claim herself a fool, but it didn't feel right to declare herself wise.

"I have a proposition for you. I will forget about the earring if you agree to bring me three things instead: the answers to three riddles. If you solve one of them, I will allow you to keep the field. If you solve two, I will set your father free. And if you solve all three..."

The king looked at Sonia, studying her. The silence stretched on forever as she waited for him to finish.

"I will make you my queen."

Her eyes widened, and her breath caught in her chest. The king had lost his mind. Or he was toying with her. Either way, she would play along. She cleared her throat. "What shall I bring you, Your Majesty?"

"Tall, it is young. Short, it is old. With life, it does glow. A breath is its foe."

"What is the second?"

"I can see nothing else when I look in its face. It will look me in the eye, and it will never lie."

"And the third?"

"If broken, it does not stop working. If touched, it may be snared. If lost, nothing will matter." He folded his hands together and leaned on one arm, flashing her an easy smile.

Sonia nodded. With so much at stake, she had expected harder riddles. If she'd had the items in question, she would have given them to him then and there. "Is there anything else, or shall I fetch these things now?"

"Alistair." The king motioned to a burly servant. "Give her the list, so she doesn't forget."

"Thank you, but that won't be necessary." She pointed to her head. "Memory."

She could recite back every word of their conversation twenty years later if needed; remembering a handful of riddles was nothing. With her Gift, she couldn't forget anything, even if she wanted to.

♛

When a servant escorted Sonia into the room the next morning, the king sat on the edge of his seat, gripping the arms of his throne. His dark eyes lit up for a moment as he looked her over, then he frowned. "Have you given up so soon?"

Sonia curtsied and smiled sweetly. She had not given up at all; she simply carried nothing where he could see. Reaching into her pocket, she pulled out a candle and held it out to him. "Tall, it is young. Short, it is old. With life, it does glow. A breath is its foe. I give you a candle."

He nodded. "You will keep your field."

Sonia handed the candle to a servant and pulled out a mirror the size of her hand, holding it up to the king. "You can see nothing else when you look in its face. It will look you in the eye, and it will never lie. I give you your reflection."

"Well done," Basil said, then turned to Alistair. "Go to the jail and inform them that George may go free."

She breathed a sigh of relief. Only one riddle left.

He turned back to Sonia. "You may accompany him. I'm sure you are eager to see your father again."

Her smile faltered briefly. "But, Your Majesty, what about the third riddle? Does your offer no longer stand?"

He froze for a moment.

Oh no. She had judged wrong. The king had been toying with her with his proposition, and she'd foolishly taken him seriously. Sonia swallowed, her mouth as hot and dry as over-baked cornbread.

His deep olive skin took on a touch of pink, and he cleared his throat. Without a trace of mockery in his voice, he asked, "Have you brought me the solution to the third riddle?"

She took a step toward the throne, and the guards on either side of Basil moved to intercept her, but he waved them off. She mentally kicked herself for acting without permission. Her pulse pounded. She didn't want to think about what might happen if her answer was wrong, but she had to take the chance. She would never starve again, and all she had to do was choose to give herself to him and hope he accepted her offering.

Sonia looked into the king's eyes. A lock of black hair fell over one, and she wanted to push it away. He was still a stranger to her, but she felt a kindred spirit in him. Someone who wouldn't ignore or dismiss her out of hand. Feelings could come later. She trusted they would. But she could choose this path now, with or without them.

Slowly, she approached him as she recited, "If broken, it does not stop working. If touched, it may be snared. If lost, nothing will matter."

Sonia held his face with both hands, the faintest tremble in her fingers.

And kissed him.

She whispered in his ear, "I give you my heart."

♛

Basil looked over at his bride and smiled. With her golden tiara and full-length gown, she carried herself like she had been born a queen. Her green silk dress matched the evergreen boughs decorating the dining room, symbols of their everlasting union. He held out her chair as she sat down gracefully.

Within a month, the wedding had been arranged, new clothing had been made, and Sonia had absorbed all the knowledge the palace tutors had thrown at her. Looking at her now, if Basil hadn't known better, he never would have guessed at her humble origins.

In the middle of the room, brightly dressed dancers moved to the rhythm of a box drum. Normally, Basil would have reveled in the sight, but the woman next to him captured all of his attention, and he gladly gave it to her. When the dancers finished a set, Sonia clapped politely, though her smile radiated enthusiasm. She reached for her newly-filled cup, and Basil felt an overwhelming urge to show off his own Gift. "May I?" He extended his hand.

She raised an eyebrow and passed the drink to him. For a moment, her delicate fingers entwined with his around the cup, turning his thoughts toward the end of the night. Her cheeks turned rosy, and warmth rose in his. He wondered if her mind had also strayed there.

Basil held the cup in both hands for a few seconds, his body warming slightly as he absorbed the energy from the liquid. He handed the cup back to her. "Well?"

Sonia took a sip of the chilled drink and gasped. "Ice? I never would have guessed. Why isn't that common knowledge?"

Basil shuddered. In his eagerness to impress her, he'd forgotten about the *incident*. "Do you remember my father, how he was known for having Ice?"

Sonia tried to hide a smile. "Do I remember?"

He shook his head. "Right. I keep forgetting that you can't forget."

"It happens all the time." She brushed a hand over his shoulder, her touch gentle. "You were saying about your father?"

Basil leaned in close and lowered his voice. "My father was arguing with a nobleman who had Fire and poor control. He expelled heat when he was angry, and when Father put a hand on his arm..."

"Their Gifts amplified each other."

He nodded somberly and feigned interest in his food, a vain attempt to hide the horror and sorrow he remembered. "It was over in seconds."

Sonia took his hand and met his gaze with soft eyes. "I'm so sorry. I shouldn't have asked. This is supposed to be a celebration."

"It's all right. It was a long time ago. I just don't want anyone getting ideas. I try my best to be a fair ruler, but it's impossible not to make enemies, and I wouldn't underestimate the lengths some men could go to."

He knew how easily desperate men could be swayed. A man with a starving family could be paid to use Fire against him. Someone out for revenge with nothing left to live for could too.

"Is that why I've never seen anyone use Fire in the palace?"

He ran his thumb over the back of her hand. "It's a precaution."

She flashed him a flirty smile and batted her eyelashes. "For a man so concerned with safety, I'm surprised you let me approach you."

Basil laughed. "Memory is a harmless Gift."

"Says the man clearly haunted by memories."

Sonia stumbled forward blindly and felt Basil's arm wrap around her waist to steady her. "Can I open my eyes yet?"

His cheek tickled against hers. "Patience, dear."

Loose rocks slid under her feet, and he tightened his hold. A rhythmic hushing sound filled her ears. "Am I allowed to guess?"

"Absolutely not. I wouldn't put it past you to be able to guess anything. I want to see you surprised for once."

"I was surprised when you offered to marry me."

He laughed. "With my imperfect memory, I could do with seeing it more than once. All right, open your eyes."

They stood at the edge of the shore in front of a canoe carved with intricate designs from a single piece of wood.

He took her hand and gestured forward. "I wanted it to be a wedding gift, but the carvings took a few extra weeks. I'm afraid none of my boatbuilders have Speed. Do you like it?"

She kissed his cheek and climbed into the boat. She'd always wanted one of her own. "It's beautiful," she breathed, running her fingertips over the polished craft. Sonia smiled and held out a hand to Basil. "What made you think to do this?"

"You told me you loved the water."

Sonia blushed as she remembered the time she had told him. "Then that's the second surprise of the day. I thought you'd have been too distracted to remember that."

Basil pushed off from the shore and jumped in the boat with a sly grin. "On the contrary, I think it helped my memory."

☙

Basil tried to think of something new to do with Sonia as the weather turned even colder and rainier, and the bay less pleasant to ride around. But his thoughts were cut short when a guard ushered two scowling men into the throne room. "These two were arguing in the middle of the market in Vaygray. They would have come to blows if we hadn't intervened."

Basil perked up. Vaygray? Sonia was from there. "What was this dispute over?"

"Both of them claim ownership of a pair of malamute pups that were found in a turkey coop."

He sighed. "Puppies? You two were ready to brawl in the street over puppies?"

"See?" one of them said, crossing his massive arms. He looked as though he could snap his neighbor like a twig. "Even the king thinks you're being ridiculous. They're mine now, Philip. Let it go."

"Please, Your Majesty," Philip said. "Just hear me out. They're important. I'm going to train them to pull my wares."

"And what are your wares?" Basil asked.

Philip grinned. "I'm glad you asked. Let me give you a demonstration." He reached into a small leather satchel hanging at his side and removed a solid glass cylinder. After a few moments, he began molding it like clay, pressing and shaping the molten glass.

Fire.

Basil's fingers dug into the arms of his throne. His heart raced. He couldn't shake the image of his father lying on the ground. He tried to steady his breathing and waved Alistair to his side. He couldn't allow these villagers to see the imminent fit that threatened to overtake him. "Guards, escort these men out of the palace."

"But what about my dogs?" Philip called out as they dragged him toward the door.

"They can stay where they are."

A few minutes later, the guards returned.

"He was holding this," one of them said as he handed the piece of glass to Basil.

He wanted to break it into a thousand pieces. A glass canoe, resembling the one he had made for Sonia. What designs Philip had finished matched the carvings on its hull. Those outings were private. Had he been spying on them? He lived in her old village. Had she been sharing the intimate details of their life together with this man? Basil told himself it was a coincidence, but it felt like a taunt nonetheless.

Sonia knocked on the door of the little log cabin. It had been months since she'd last set foot inside. She would have preferred to keep it that way. Memories of starvation and desperation would never go away, but at least at the palace, they were easier to drown out with happy ones: Basil's dimpled smile when she said "I do"; his arms around her as he nuzzled her neck the next morning, tickling her with his stubble and laughing along with her giggles; sweet notes written with frost on her mirror every morning.

Here at the cabin, everything around her spoke of hunger pains, of being forced to swallow her pride and beg. She closed her eyes and took a deep breath. This one visit wouldn't ruin her day.

Her father opened the door and waved her inside. He tipped his head at her guards. "Can they stay outside? I have a guest."

She asked the men to wait and followed her father into their old home. "Why couldn't you come to the palace to see me?" she asked as she closed the door behind them.

"Because I'm not welcome there," a familiar voice said.

She turned to the man warming himself by a fire he had no doubt started with his bare hands. "Philip?" It had been less than a year since she'd seen him, but it felt like longer.

"Sonia," he said, opening his arms to invite a hug, then abruptly sweeping into a bow. "I mean, Your Majesty." He shook his head. "I still can't believe you married the king after what he did to George."

She scowled. How dare he. "Father made a choice. He may have had to spend a few days in jail, but did he tell you that he also owns this whole farm now? Basil has been more than generous with both of us."

"But you refused me after I helped you? You wouldn't have lived through the winter without me. What of my generosity?" Philip gestured to himself with both hands.

"Kindness doesn't entitle you to anyone. He offered me what you never could."

He scoffed. "A palace and jewels?"

She crossed her arms. Did he really think her so shallow? "Respect. Honor. Someone who cares what I think."

With a groan, he threw his hands in the air. "I don't understand you."

No. Philip never did understand her, which was why they would have made a poor match. No matter how many times she had told him, he couldn't see it. She felt no need to explain herself yet again. "I doubt you're here just to disparage my choice of husband. What is this about?"

"He needs your help to bring a matter to the king," her father said, shooting Philip a look that said, *Behave yourself.*

"I see." Part of Sonia wanted to leave Philip to his own problems—why did every conversation have to become an argument?—but her curiosity outweighed her irritation. "What is the matter?"

Philip took a seat by the fire. "River had a litter a few weeks ago, and two of her pups escaped. Nicolas found them in his turkey coop and says they're his now."

She nodded. "That sounds simple enough. Why do you need my help?"

"Because the king had me thrown out of court! He let Nicolas keep the dogs."

"Thrown out of court? Philip, I'm not sure I can help you if you've angered him." She stuck her hands to her hips. "What did you do?"

He put his hands in the air. "I swear, I don't know. He asked me why I needed the dogs, and I began to demonstrate my glass-work. The next thing I knew, he had me thrown out."

Of course. Philip's Fire. But that didn't mean he deserved to lose his dogs. He trained them young to carry his glass to market, and losing two would cost him time and money.

Sonia shook her head. She couldn't send him back to court, and she didn't have the authority to undermine Basil's ruling. But she had to help. She had known Philip since they were children, and without his help, she would have starved last winter. She owed him.

"I have an idea, but you cannot tell anyone I helped you. If anybody asks, you came up with it yourself. Understand?"

Philip nodded vigorously. "Anything."

♛

Basil looked out the window of his study to see what all the commotion was. It sounded like a parade, with people shouting and laughing. Through the rain-soaked glass, he could see a crowd gathered around the middle of the market. In the center, a young man had stuck posts in the ground and was stringing lines between them. Cloth overflowed the basket at his feet, and he took pieces out one by one to pin to the line.

"Alistair," Basil said, "find out what that man is doing."

He waited and watched Alistair run outside, speak briefly with the man, and run back.

"He says he's hanging his laundry."

Basil sighed. "Obviously. I want to know why he's hanging his laundry outside."

"I'll go find out." Alistair turned back toward the door.

"Never mind. I'm coming with you this time."

He wanted a closer look, and playing courier with Alistair was clearly going to take all day.

Basil's guards made a path for him through the crowd until he could see the crazed laundryman. People fell silent and bowed as he passed. They stared wide-eyed at the king and the strange man, not in fear, but in anticipation. What could be a more interesting spectacle?

The man turned around as Basil drew close, and he gasped as he recognized his face: the glassmith. "You! Why are you hanging laundry in the street? Have you lost your mind?"

Philip announced for the whole crowd to hear, "If dogs can hatch from turkey eggs, I can dry my clothes in the rain."

The crowd erupted with laughter, and he pinned another shirt to the line.

Basil seethed. "Who told you to do this?"

"I don't have any idea what you're talking about, Your Majesty."

Bullshit. The man wasn't this witty the last time he saw him. "You couldn't have come up with this idea on your own. Who told you to hang these clothes outside?"

"Nobody. I thought it up all by myself."

Basil had enough. Just being in proximity to Philip made him nervous, and the crowd didn't help. The farce needed to end. He motioned for Alistair to step in.

Alistair stretched his neck and cracked his knuckles, flexing his huge arms. "The king asked you a question."

"But I promise—"

Alistair grabbed Philip and effortlessly hoisted him above his head.

Philip cringed and whined. "Queen Sonia! It was her idea. Please, put me down."

Basil felt a pit in his stomach. She wouldn't do that to him. She couldn't. Not for someone with Fire. "You're lying again."

"No. Please. I'm not lying anymore. Please, just let me go."

Basil waved his hand, and Alistair put Philip down.

"You will spend two nights in jail for this stunt. Then, you will take your dogs and go home. And if you *ever* speak to my queen again, the sentence will be much longer." Basil turned back to the palace. He needed to talk to Sonia.

♛

Sonia stepped back to check the flower arrangement one more time. A quiet evening alone. They usually dined with the rest of court, but Basil had promised her days ago that this night would be theirs.

She smiled as she heard the door open. "Basil, my dear, how was your—"

"How could you?" His words were choked. "How could you betray me?"

Sonia looked up from the flowers.

Basil's face contorted, his eyes shining.

"Betray you? What do you—"

"I was humiliated today by a man with a clothesline, and I'm told it was your idea."

She reached for his hand, but he pulled away. "Basil, it was never meant to hurt you. I just wanted to help an old friend."

"An old friend? Are you sure about that?" He held out a glass canoe. "He made this. It would seem he's more than an old friend."

The boat looked like hers, but how? Philip must have been spying on her. He had assumed himself entitled to her before, but she'd never imagined that he wouldn't leave her be after she married. "I didn't know. He never told me what he made. All he said was that you turned him away, and I owed him a debt." She took a step toward Basil.

He put a hand up. "I want you to leave."

Sonia couldn't breathe.

"Return to your father's cottage, and don't come back." His ragged voice sounded the way her chest felt.

Tears stung her eyes as she tried in vain to blink them back. Her world shattered. Hadn't they been happy together? The heart she had offered him so freely was being ripped from her chest. She took off her necklace and bracelets and began removing her earrings. The clink of the metal in her hands reverberated in the silence of their room.

"What are you doing?"

"These don't belong to me. I came to you with nothing, and I will leave with nothing."

His features softened. "I won't send you away empty-handed. I'll let you take one thing with you. Whatever you treasure most, whatever is dearest to you, you may take with you."

She looked down at the table laid out for them and nodded. A drop fell onto her plate. "One last dinner before I leave?" she asked softly, then met his gaze. "You already promised me this night."

Basil sighed and pulled up a chair. "One last dinner."

They ate in silence. Sonia soberly watched as Basil refilled his wine glass again and again until he'd emptied the bottle, then opened another. He stumbled to the bed and passed out without so much as a "goodbye".

Sonia stepped into the hallway. "Alistair, I have a task for you."

Basil groaned. He couldn't bring himself to open his eyes. His head pounded, and he knew the morning light would only make it worse. Even the sheets felt coarse on his skin. This had to be the worst hangover he'd ever had.

He heard the sounds of footsteps and smelled fresh cornbread. Maybe breakfast would help. "Alistair, bring me some water."

Alistair didn't reply.

Basil squinted his eyes open. Who'd moved his bed so close to the window? And for that matter, since when did he have a ground-level view of the trees?

He jolted upright.

The narrow bed he sat in occupied the corner of a small, plain room. Someone was walking around outside the door.

"Who's there? Where am I?"

The door opened, and Sonia entered, carrying a tray of food and smiling. "Good morning, love. How did you like my bed?"

"But what am I doing here?"

She sat next to him and took his hand. "You told me to take whatever I treasured the most, and there is no treasure dearer to my heart than you."

Eyes and heart full to bursting, he smiled. He took her face with both hands and kissed her. Basil was ready to take his wife home.

I LOVED YOU TOMORROW

an original love story

It had been three years since Moira had Seen the future for the first time. The unbidden visions no longer startled her. When they came, she took note and carried on with her day—usually.

Mother had tasked her with inspecting one of the guest rooms before their next visitor, and everything looked to be in order. She pulled back the sea blue brocade drapes and checked the cedar window frame. No leaks, no creaking hinges. No wear or fading on the drapery. The desk and chair felt sturdy, and a sufficient supply of paper and ink were left on the maple surface. What about the mattress? She sat on the edge of the bed, then leaned back, letting her fingers brush against the raised texture of the comforter.

An Elgathan man with strikingly blue eyes appeared to her. Strange. She'd never seen him before, and all her visions so far had featured people she knew. The man stood in this room, leaning over the bed a foot or so to her left. Moira turned her head to see what he might be looking at, only to see herself lying back in the same position she was in now.

Her future self's face looked a tad more angular, her body more voluptuous. Moira glanced down at her current bosom and shrugged. It was nice to see that she'd eventually finish filling out.

The man smiled knowingly at older Moira. She smirked back, hooked a finger through the neck of his shirt, and slowly pulled him closer.

Moira had never been kissed before. She'd seen servants and farmers sneaking together in darkened corners during festivals and holidays, but not like this. This was the embrace of a couple who was not hiding: deliberate, unhurried, and unabashed. Heat flooded up from her chest to her cheeks as she watched them, his lingering touches almost palpably imaginable on her present body as she saw them on her older counterpart. Moira blinked, but closing her eyes was useless against visions.

A knock sounded at the door, heard only in her head, not with her ears. The couple both groaned. Older Moira giggled. "It's worse than at home."

The man kissed her forehead and rolled onto his back to her left. "Come in," he sighed loudly.

Mother opened the door. "Sorry to interrupt, but…"

The vision faded away.

Moira stared at the ceiling and focused on breathing steadily. That was the most vivid and concrete thing she'd ever Seen. She put a hand to her still warm cheek. That wouldn't be the last vision she would see like that. A dam had been breached, and a flood was sure to follow. She had Seen the man she would marry.

FIVE YEARS LATER

Rhonwin set down his book as Faye popped her head in the door. She thought louder than anyone he knew, and he'd heard her halfway down the hallway. "Pettilord Nevin's daughter has arrived, and Father has sent for me," he said flatly.

Faye pouted. "I was going to say it."

He smirked. "You don't need to, now."

Fine, then. I won't tell you that she looks to be your age and wasn't wearing a ring—oh, no. Really?

Rhonwin laughed and patted her shoulder. "An admirable effort, Faye, but thanks for the information." He would have to work with her more on redirecting her thoughts.

He took a quick peek in the mirror. No unruly hair nor food in his teeth? Good enough. Unless he changed his clothing into something fancier, primping wouldn't be worth the effort. He had yet to hear a woman's opinion of him change on account of it.

Faye followed him down the hallway and a flight of stairs. Rhonwin paused outside the door to Father's office. The thoughts of those inside carried better than their voices but still sounded fuzzy. If he tried harder to Listen, he could have heard them clearly.

His little sister leaned against the smooth cedar wall, an ear cocked toward the door.

It was bad enough that Father had him invading the private thoughts of their people. She didn't need to dive headfirst into the muck with him. "No eavesdropping," he whispered, shooing her away.

"I wouldn't have to if I were invited in." She put a hand on her hip. "Besides, it's not eavesdropping if I'm not really trying."

"That's not how it—never mind." She was going to put her ear to the door as soon as he walked in, no matter what he said, and now was not a time for debate.

Faye leaned back against the wall, grinning. *I win.*

Brat. That Hearing amplified sound instead of thoughts didn't make her actions less invasive. Rhonwin shook his head and walked in.

A statuesque woman faced Father, her back to the entrance. Ashy brunette silk twisted around her nape and flowed halfway down her back. The hem of her fine teal dress grazed the tops of tall muddy boots.

Perfect timing. Father gestured to the woman. "Rhonwin, I would like you to meet Pettilord Nevin's daughter, Moira."

She turned to Rhonwin, and as her gaze met his, he saw a flash of his own blue eyes reflected in her dark ones. *Great Giver. It's* him*!*

He had heard more than a few women his age admire him—and admire many other men—before but never with so much awe. To her credit, if he didn't have Listening, he would never have guessed her reaction; she kept her expression politely neutral.

Rhonwin held out his hand. "A pleasure to meet you."

Finally... He's even more handsome in person. "The pleasure is mine." Moira rested her hand in his and curtsied. In vivid color, he saw himself from the outside. The other Rhonwin stood in front of his bedroom window, holding Moira tenderly, both of them dressed in wedding finery. He kissed her slowly, deeply. *My love...*

If her hand had been a burning coal, he wouldn't have dropped it faster. Love? He didn't know her. And she certainly had no business knowing what his bedroom looked like.

No! This is all wrong. How can he be so cold? This isn't like him. Not my sweet—

"You summoned me for a reason?" Rhonwin needed to make her think of something—anything—else.

Father raised an eyebrow. *As if you didn't Listen the answer out of one of us already.*

Rhonwin breathed a barely audible, "No," that only Father could Hear.

"There is an important project which Pettilord Nevin lacks the sufficient funds to support. I need you to accompany Moira back to Losuno to act as my deputy and oversee the use of Atmos's assets."

That sounded mildly unpleasant but not unreasonable. He could endure a few hours travel with her then deal with Nevin directly in Losuno. "What is the project?"

Father motioned to Moira. "Well, it was your idea."

Rhonwin looked toward her again, careful to avoid eye contact this time.

"A few weeks ago," she said, "a young man with Fire accidentally burned down three shops in our market. Thankfully, nobody was injured, but incidents like that happen too often. Too many of our youth are inadequately trained, and few can afford to send their children as far as Meria or Iverish for training. A school in Losuno would serve all of Atmos."

Father chimed in. "The two of you will choose a plot, architect, and builders. In the meantime, find a temporary location and gather teachers."

The two of them? "I won't be working with Pettilord Nevin?"

Don't be rude, Father thought.

Moira crossed her arms. *What did I do to offend him so?* "My father wants the project completed quickly. He's delegated it to me."

Great. They would have to work together for months—at least.

Father stood. "You depart tomorrow. The purse I'm providing should last at least two months. Send reports weekly." *And the other reports as well.* He put his hands on Rhonwin's and Moira's shoulders. "I have another meeting elsewhere, but I'd like you both to get started right away. Please, continue to use my office."

Moira curtsied. "Thank you, Lord Flinor."

Rhonwin tensed as the door clicked shut behind Father. What should he say to her?

What do I say?

She had a right to know that her thoughts weren't private around him, but the backlash to such a revelation was always ugly. On the bright side, she seemed to have moved past fawning over him, though he feared the panic he was going to cause would be much, much worse. Perhaps if they got some of the business out of the way first, he could save it for the end and walk away when—

"Why do you hate me?" she asked.

"I beg your pardon?" As much as he understood the question, the bluntness caught him off guard.

Moira glared at him. "You know nothing more than my name and my station, and yet you have looked at me with nothing but disgust. What about me do you find so offensive?"

Rhonwin inhaled sharply. She had lost her chance for him to be delicate. "What do I find offensive? Oh, I don't know... Maybe it's a stranger imagining my bedroom or fantasizing about me in it. Maybe it's her thinking of me as her lover. That is quite the double standard you have, madam, judging me for *my* response to *you*."

Shit... Listening? Her olive skin bloomed dark pink. "I'm so sorry. I didn't know you could hear all that."

"And see. That visual when I touched your hand was...uh..."

I want to crawl into a hole and die. "That wasn't—you weren't meant to see that yet. I would've been more careful had I known that you would be you."

Rhonwin tilted his head. "Yet? If you knew I would be me? What does any of that nonsense mean?"

"It means I've already revealed more of your future than you're ready for." *It would have been handy to foresee this scenario. Stupid unpredictable visions.*

He took a step back. "That bedroom image wasn't a fantasy? It was supposed to be the future?" Being a seer didn't preclude daydreams, but that somehow seemed an unlikely possibility.

Well, he knows enough now. Might as well just say it. "Yes, Rhonwin. I'm your future wife."

A chill ran up his spine. "You mean *possible* future wife." Even he knew not all visions were equal. Some were definite, some only possible, and others had elements of both. Seers could instinctively distinguish between them, but Rhonwin could not, no matter how vivid the second-hand image was.

"No. It wasn't that kind of vision." *But I wish it were now.*

"It is now." He stalked to the door.

Where is he going?

"To pack. We can discuss our real task tomorrow on the way to Losuno. In the meantime, forget about that vision. It's not going to happen."

Faye pounced on Rhonwin the moment the door closed behind him. "Have you lost your mind?"

He rolled his eyes and pressed past her, determined to return to his room. "That conversation was not intended for your ears."

"Don't walk away. You need to go back to her."

"Stay out of this, Faye."

She flicked his ear.

"Ow. Hey!" He ducked and glared back at her.

"Do you know what most people would give to find the love of their life so easily?"

"She's not the love of my life. I don't even know her."

"You have a whole lifetime for that."

He took the steps up two at a time. "I'm not asking a stranger to marry me, no matter what vision she's had."

Faye scurried to catch up. "At least offer her a ribbon. You know she'll accept."

"Absolutely not." Why would he give a ribbon of intent to a woman he had no intentions with?

"Why not? You said she's a stranger. What better way to get to know her than to court her?"

"I don't want to know her. I want to do my duty to Atmos, nothing more."

You're impossible. "That assignment from Father isn't your only duty to Atmos."

Rhonwin stepped into his bedroom. "It isn't your concern," he said as he shut Faye out.

Fool. Her footsteps receded outside. *It's a wonder he even has a soul mate to reject when he's...*

When would she learn to butt out? He needed to marry eventually, but he was entitled to do so on his own terms, in his own time.

҂

The next morning, Rhonwin stood next to the dogcart, reluctant to take his seat. With a cramped, two-hour ride ahead, he wanted to stand while he could.

The driver knelt and rubbed the two lead dogs behind their ears, huffing and humming at them. *Who are my good boys today?*

Animal Speakers had the most boring thoughts, but Rhonwin would still rather Listen to him than Moira, who emerged from the manor.

Don't think. Don't think. Don't think. Don't think... She avoided looking at him and slid into the cart.

Ah, no. Two hours of that wouldn't be irritating at all. He gingerly sat beside her. Should he say something? Which would be worse: this repetition or all her thoughts focused on him?

40

...Don't think. Chapter one...

Wait—what?

He glanced over at the open book in Moira's lap. She'd found a workaround on her own. Clever. Even if she'd picked the driest story in the world, Listening to her read was infinitely preferable to the thoughts he'd expected.

Rhonwin relaxed as the cart pulled them away.

❦

Losuno came into view piece by piece, red and yellow wooden buildings peeking through the cedars in tiny clusters. After half a mile, the clusters fused into blocks with planked sidewalks along the streets. A small manor loomed farther ahead at the crest of a hill. The thoughts and sounds of townsfolk out and about grew louder in the town proper—loud enough to drown out any single person's thoughts if Rhonwin tuned her out.

"Moira."

She started. "Yes...?" She slowly closed the book and turned to him.

"We need to put this vision...mess behind us to accomplish our task, but I must know: was the vision...was it new? Had you seen that before yesterday?"

She stifled a laugh. "New? Giver, no. It's been, oh...five years, at least, since it first came to me." *And it wasn't even the first of its kind.*

Five years? Five months would have sounded too long. He cringed. "And, how many people have you shared it with?"

"In the manner you saw it? Nobody. But I did tell my mother about it. Why do you ask?"

"I'd rather not repeat our introduction— Wait. You told *your mother* about that?"

She rolled her eyes. "It's not as if I recounted every lingering touch in lascivious detail," she said in a mock-seductive voice and wiggled her eyebrows. She laughed. "I just told her that I'd seen the man I'd one day marry...and I may have told her what you looked like."

Rhonwin groaned. In his own family, his blue eyes were the only evidence left of a Vistan ancestor. Faye often teased that his hair was light as well, but it clearly still qualified as a shade of brown, and he'd avoided the pasty skin.

"Losuno's an old border town. Any chance blue-eyed Elgathan men are common here?" he asked.

"Probably more so than in most of the kingdom, but no, sorry, I wouldn't say 'common.' Nevertheless, I wouldn't worry too much. Mother won't be home for another week or two. She's visiting a friend. I'll write and explain to her before she returns."

"Thank you."

Moira shook her head. "It's nothing. You're right about not wanting a repeat of our introduction. It was humiliating enough the first time."

Rhonwin looked away. The fleeting pang of guilt wouldn't elicit an apology from him. He wasn't that foolish.

They neared the manor now, and several people waited outside. Pettilord Nevin stood out in front, conspicuous in an embroidered blue jacket and brown pants, with a large silver magnifying glass hanging from a chain around his neck.

Moira and Rhonwin hopped out almost before the cart stopped. "Father," she said, "may I present Rhonwin, our future Lord of Atmos." *And should-have-been future other things as well.*

Rhonwin inhaled sharply. He already missed the crowded streets just downhill. Normally, he found too many thoughts overwhelming, but not today.

"Rhonwin, this is my father, Pettilord Nevin."

The two men each gave a half-bow to one another. Nevin ushered them inside. "I would love to give you a tour of the house myself, but I think it would be better to let Moira do the honors. You may set to work as soon as you are ready, and remember that my staff is at your disposal." He gave another half-bow and left Rhonwin and Moira alone in the entry hall.

"Shall we?" She motioned to a doorway.

"After you." Rhonwin followed her just inside a hallway to a flight of stairs.

"Down that way are storerooms. The kitchen is at the end."

He smiled. "I see you started with—"

The most important room, she finished in unison with him. She blushed and ducked into the stairwell. *You can't do that, Moira. He can hear you.*

He climbed after her. At the top of the stairs, she turned left and stopped in front of a door.

"This is the guest hall. It's empty at the moment, but you can use this room." She opened it, gesturing for him to walk in.

The bedroom was smaller than his own but well furnished. Rich blue brocade draped the windows and covered a large bed in the center. The

42

maple headboard and desk featured matching carvings in a repeated bear motif. Rhonwin rested a hand on the foot of the bed.

It's so surreal to see him here... *No. Don't think of that.* Moira put a hand to her reddened cheek.

"I can only see pictures of your thoughts if I'm touching you. Whatever you saw, only your panic over it is drawing my attention."

"I'm sorry. I'm trying, but seeing you in here—" She looked away from the bed. "I can't unSee the visions I've had."

Much as he appreciated the effort, he couldn't let her continue this way. He crossed the room and stuck his head into the hallway. Satisfied that it was empty, he closed the door.

She gasped. "What are you doing?"

He crossed his arms. "We're never going to accomplish anything until you learn to control your thoughts."

How can I not think of him when he's right in front of me? She shook her head. "This is pointless. I'll just ask my father to assign someone else to work with you."

He was taken aback. "You would do that?"

She shrugged. "I would rather finish what I started, and Father will pitch a fit about me shirking my duties, but yes, I will."

"Why?"

Because I love you, you fool. "I told you, our fate together is inevitable. But marriage isn't a guarantee of happiness. I don't want you to resent me any more than you clearly do now. You've made it quite obvious that you want to be as far from me as possible, so I will give you the time and space you need." Moira's voice wavered with her last few words. She turned and started for the door.

"Wait."

She paused, hand on the knob.

He still wasn't ready to accept her vision, and she was right about him, but he couldn't let her do this. She hadn't set all this in motion on purpose, and she was trying her best to make amends.

"You don't have to do that," he said. "It isn't fair of me to expect you to punish yourself for my sake. Especially not when I could teach you to redirect your thoughts."

But trying not to think of you only makes me think of you more.

"Because that's not how it works. You don't actively avoid a thought. You focus on something else."

She let go of the door and turned around. *I don't know what else to think of now.*

"That's okay. It's good that you're communicating by thought; keep doing that. Now, what made you want to build a school?"

Moira closed her eyes. *The children with new Gifts don't know how to use them.*

Rhonwin stepped closer, a few inches from her. "Be more specific."

That boy lost control of his Fire.

"Look at me. Tell me about the boy."

She opened her eyes. *You're so close...*

"I know. Focus. If you can focus through this, you can handle working with me."

The boy. He was warming a cold loaf of bread in his hands, but the bread caught fire instantly. He didn't know he couldn't burn himself, so he dropped it. Three houses burned before the town could put out the flames.

Rhonwin offered his hand. "Tell me where we should start with the project."

I can do this. Moira slowly put her hand in his. *We need to assess what Gifts we need trainers for and send out a call for volunteers.*

Rhonwin smiled and let go of her hand. "We're ready to work now."

❧

It was too early in the morning for this. Rhonwin ran a hand through his hair and stared at the blank paper waiting on his desk. It was best to write his reports and send them before Moira joined him for their day's work, but he loathed writing them. The progress report was fine enough. Distributing the call for volunteers had cost very little, and checking maps for locations had cost only time. Father would be pleased.

But the other report... Neither Nevin nor Moira had thought anything of note—at least, not anything he wanted to repeat to Father. He had an uncanny way of knowing when Rhonwin failed to provide details, but he could not reveal Moira's visions. What if Father had the same reaction as Faye? Rhonwin couldn't report that they hadn't thought anything at all. That wasn't believable; there was always something to report. Unfortunately, he'd been too distracted to remember whatever that something was.

He sighed. The progress report would have to do for now. He'd try to focus more today and find something to write to Father before dinner tonight.

So quiet. Did he fall back asleep? Moira's thoughts drifted through his closed door.

He gingerly walked over and opened it. He raised an eyebrow. What did she want?

Dressed only in a nightgown with a thick blanket wrapped around her, she held out a heaping plate of food. *Can I come in?*

His stomach rumbled. He stepped aside and closed the door behind her. "What's this about?"

"I was just up early, and I didn't feel like waiting for breakfast. On the way to the kitchen, I saw the light under your door, so I got some for you as well."

He took a strawberry from the plate. "You don't think it's a tad inappropriate?"

She scoffed. "I'm offering you food, not my body." *Maybe I'm not the only one struggling with my thoughts.* She set the plate on his desk and walked back to the door. "You're welcome, by the way."

"I didn't mean to imply—you don't have to abandon your breakfast over one remark."

Moira smiled. "With your appetite, I wouldn't dream of coming between you and that plate." She winked and gave a tiny curtsy. *Besides, I already ate downstairs. Enjoy,* she thought as she backed out the door.

Rhonwin scratched his head. Her timing was impeccable. Did she know about his spying for Father? Was she trying to bribe him into reporting favorably? He picked a piece of cornbread from the plate. No. He'd have heard her think so. This was simple hospitality—well, hospitality at any rate—nothing about her was simple.

❧

Moira ushered Rhonwin into the library. It was afternoon, and he still had no idea what to write to Father. He hadn't seen Nevin all day, and Moira had been too busy meeting with volunteers all morning for idle thought. Rhonwin would have to prompt one of them. He grimaced. It was easier to justify the spying to himself when he didn't have to actively dig for information. Though, he had to admit it was his own fault for both trying to tune her thoughts out and driving her to hide them.

Moira pulled a map off the shelf and unrolled it on the table. All of Losuno lay before them.

Rhonwin cleared his throat. "About this morning... I shouldn't have been so rude. Thank you for the breakfast."

She shrugged, not looking up from the map. "It's fine. I knew the food would improve your mood."

So she was buttering him up. "How did you know my mood needed improving?"

"It was the crack of dawn." *You hate early mornings.*

"That's all? No other reason?"

Moira look up at him, then leaned back against the table and crossed her arms. "Do I need another reason?" *What are you looking for?* Her eyes were full of confusion, not suspicion.

Unless she was more skilled at deception than anyone he'd ever met, her motives were truly as simple as she claimed. He rubbed the back of his neck. "No...I—We should get back to work."

"You had that same look this morning. Is something wrong?" she asked gently.

"I thought you were trying to..."

What? Seduce you?

"...bribe me."

She tilted her head. *Bribe?*

"My father has me report thoughts that might be of interest to him," Rhonwin blurted. Something about her earnest concern compelled him to.

"I'd be more surprised if you didn't. Now, if that's all—"

He gaped. "I just told you that I'm spying for your lord."

"I know." She clapped a hand to his shoulder. "And I don't care." *It's not who you really are.* "I can give you some information to pass along to him after we check this map, if that's what you need."

"This doesn't bother you?"

"All I have to hide from you or Lord Flinor are the things that *you* don't wish to see. And frankly, I'm more interested in your thoughts on this map right now."

Rhonwin shook his head. "Right—sorry—the reason I'm here. Now, where are the clearings?"

Moira leaned over the map and pointed to a far corner. "Some of the biggest ones are a long way from the manor..." She moved her fingers gracefully across the surface as she spoke.

He stole a glance at her determined countenance before following her hand. In more pleasant circumstances, he'd have found that highly attractive, but he could not, would not, allow himself to fall in love with her.

A week later, Rhonwin waited patiently for the pettilord to finish looking over their current plans. Nevin crossed his arms and raised a skeptical eyebrow at Moira. "You want to use our great hall?"

She put her hands up. "Just until we can move into a permanent location."

"And what about the danger to our manor?"

"Fire, Ice, Strength, Speed, and Flight will all be practiced in the yard," Rhonwin assured him. "We'll build the necessary facilities for practicing those Gifts first on whatever plot we choose."

Nevin stroked his chin. "When are you planning to start? Do you have any tutors lined up?"

Moira handed him a list. "We have sixteen. The fourteen most common Gifts all have volunteers here in Losuno."

And the other two? Nevin thought.

"Moira and I will fill in until we can find others with Seeing or Listening willing to move here."

Nevin narrowed his eyes at Rhonwin. *I told you not to do that.*

Rhonwin nodded. "Sorry, force of habit—but we can start as soon as you give the word."

"There are Gifts rarer than yours. Are you not serving them?"

Moira took the list back. "Not to start with. We haven't checked all of Atmos, but Losuno has no current need for training in the rarest Gifts."

"It isn't worth it to hire them either," Rhonwin added. "For the cost of finding and paying one tutor to come here and stay one year, we could pay all the expenses to send three children to school in Meria."

"And not every Gift has a pressing need," Moira said. "With passive Gifts, teaching is more about learning to cope than control. Listening, Seeing, Hearing, any of the Sights—there's little to mentor with those. We temporarily hire them for a week or two as needed and use the extra funds for hiring more teachers for active Gifts or buying more equipment."

Nevin looked at the two of them. He shook his head and smiled. "I can't believe you put this all together in two weeks. This stage should've taken you a month, at least. I should find more projects to pair you on."

I can think of one... Moira glanced at Rhonwin. *Sorry, that slipped right past me.*

"It's fine," he mouthed back. She had rarely let her thoughts stray around him since he'd taught her to redirect. He wouldn't hold this one against her. Truth be told, the comment would've been hard to ignore even without her vision.

"What else are you working on today?" Nevin asked.

"Rhonwin found a possible location out past Beppley Creek. We're going to survey it," Moira said.

"Just be careful. The woods are thick out there. I want you both to come back in one piece."

Moira smiled. "Not to worry; we will."

਩

Rhonwin turned over his shovel and inspected the fresh dirt. "Seems dry enough up here. The builders will know better, but I think the top of this hill could support a stone structure."

Moira crouched beside him. "Oh, yes. Much better than the marsh down below. The trees are sparser here too, so it'll be easier to clear." She stood back up. *The view should be spectacular from the top, once it's built.*

He straightened up and dusted his hands. "I wonder...would you be able to See what the finished building would look like?"

She rolled her eyes. "Oh, now you're interested in my visions?" Her eyebrows raised as she tilted her head and planted a hand on her hip.

"Well, even a possibility would be interesting here, don't you think?"

I prefer more defined fates myself. "It doesn't really work that way. I can't make myself See. The visions come of their own accord."

That wasn't very convenient. He'd hoped it might work differently than Listening, but he should've expected such similar Gifts to work the same. "You don't control it at all?"

"If I touch something or someone of significance to a particular vision, I can See it again." *You won't like where this is going.*

Why did everything come back to their supposed future together? He scoffed. "Are those the only visions you have? Why don't you ever share ones that don't concern me?"

She put her hands out. "Because they don't concern you...?" *If you ask a stupid question...*

"Oh." He guessed it was a bit selfish to assume that. "Well, has the school been in any of your visions?"

"Not really. The visions can get sort of...fuzzy when children are involved. I cannot know someone's Gift before they receive it, so the visions fade in and out at moments that would reveal that. But I do have a good imagination. The school is easy enough to picture." She offered him her hand. "You can Listen in, if you'd like."

He stared at her open palm. Dappled sunlight danced across her slender fingers, inviting him to play. Rhonwin slid his hand over Moira's and stepped closer to view the landscape beside her.

She showed him a large rounded interior. The details were nowhere near as vivid as her visions of the future but solid enough to replace the trees closest to them. River rock lined the floor and walls, which sloped into a domed ceiling with a hole in the center. A steel door and steel-shuttered windows opened to the forest. Moira pulled Rhonwin to where the door would be, and a path appeared, leading down the hill to a longer cedar building.

She grinned. *Want to look inside?*

He nodded eagerly, unwilling to break her thoughts with spoken words. Together, they ran down the path and through the doorway to the next imaginary interior. A large hall occupied the center with several rooms on either side. She walked him to the back of the hall, and the wall disappeared to reveal a small library.

Wouldn't it be beautiful? Moira turned and smiled, walking backward now.

As her eyes met his, Rhonwin couldn't help smiling in return. The way her nose crinkled softened his defenses, and he quickened his pace, closing the distance between them. She backed against a tree. The buildings disappeared. He stretched his free hand out over her shoulder to brace against his forward momentum. She put a steadying hand to his side, letting it linger as he stopped almost nose to nose with her. They shared a timid laugh. A glossy brown curtain of hair fell across the right side of her face. Without thinking, he let go of her hand to brush it back. She lightly tilted her head to his hand, and his fingers grazed the lush, smooth skin of her cheek. He had spent so much effort keeping her at arm's length, he hadn't before noticed the wide set of her cheeks as she smiled, the delicate curve of her nose, the graceful arch of her brow, the gentle fullness of her lips... He inched closer, a breath away from her.

Just kiss me already.

He wanted to. What was more surprising, the yearning didn't feel new, but rather like the awakening of a long-dormant desire. Not a desire. A need.

As he gently touched his lips to hers, she kissed him vigorously. She held nothing back, pulling him closer and drawing him into her earnest elation. Her fingers raked through his hair. He let go of the tree and slipped his hand around her waist. Clutching at her, breathing in her warm floral perfume, he implored her mouth with the tip of his tongue, and she obliged without hesitation. Her ardor melded with his own, their every sensation and emotion intersecting until he did not know where he ended and she began.

Perfect.

Perfect? Rhonwin broke the kiss.

Moira smiled. "I knew your embrace would be wonderful"—she nuzzled his nose—"but you're even more glorious than I imagined." *Kiss me again.*

He tore himself away. What had he been thinking? He hadn't. He'd lost his mind, and now he'd ruined everything. He turned a few paces away and ran a hand over his face. What would he do? "I'm sorry," he said huskily. "I have to go."

Rhonwin... Moira's hand grazed his as he fled, leaving him with a flash of confusion and sorrow. *No. Please...*

He ran, ignoring her protests. She did not give chase and quickly faded behind him, but he did not stop, not even through town. Let the villagers stare. He needed to clear his head.

Obviously, he could no longer trust his own self-control. Shame seared him for letting his urges overtake reason. Even now, he could still feel her lithe body close to him, feel her responding to his touch. His baser instincts screamed: he was running the wrong way!

Perhaps he would have given in even more easily had he not known of her expectations. But perhaps their encounter would not have been so exquisite without them. He'd delighted in her openness. She hadn't just allowed him entry; she'd invited him into herself, yearned to share herself with him. It was terrifying and satisfying and beautiful...and wrong. He couldn't continue to give her false hope. He needed to remove himself. Not just from the woods. From the whole situation. He could develop a plausible explanation on the cart ride home. If he packed quickly, he might be able to make it there before dark.

When he reached the relative safety of his room, Rhonwin leaned against the closed door to catch his breath. He damp shirt clung to him, suffocating him. He ripped it off and threw in at the bed with a growl.

Deep breaths.

He slid down to the floor. Letting his emotions spiral would only make things worse.

A few minutes later, content with his more level head, he picked out a new shirt and cleaned himself up as best he could with a washcloth and basin of cold water. Asking for a real bath would have meant more human interaction than he wanted right now. He dressed himself methodically and began packing, double checking every corner to be sure he'd leave nothing behind, no excuses for anyone to track him down later.

Light footsteps approached down the hall, but no audible thoughts accompanied them. If it was Moira, Rhonwin hoped she was redirecting to give him space as she passed to her own room.

A knock on the door shattered that hope.

"Go away," he called.

"No." *I'm opening this door in five seconds, whether you're ready or not.*

He threw another shirt into his bag. "Leave me be, Moira."

The door creaked open and shut, but he ignored it.

"Rhonwin, what's wrong?" She put a hand on his shoulder.

He withdrew and spun on his heels. "I made a mistake. I'm sorry."

"Sorry?" Her red-rimmed eyes narrowed. "You left me, alone, in the woods."

He looked at his packing, avoiding her gaze. "I should never have dallied with you, but I won't tempt you anymore."

She stepped between him and the bag. "I don't understand. After a kiss like that, you cannot deny the attraction between us, and destiny is on our side. Why must you fight it?"

"My life is mine. I will not be controlled by visions."

She scowled. "Lies."

"I beg your pardon! Lies?"

"Yes, lies. Telling them to yourself doesn't change what they are. This isn't about defiance. If it were, you wouldn't obey your father—and mine—without question. I don't see defiance in your eyes. I saw fear when we met, and I see it now." She approached him slowly, and gently asked, "What are you so afraid of, my love? What makes you run from me?"

"You say we're destined for each other. But what I see is perfection. It's in your vision, in your thoughts. Everything is so lovely and ideal."

"Of course, it is. You're seeing yourself through my eyes."

He shook his head. "But I cannot be the man you expect me to be. I am not perfect. I will fall from the lofty heights you see for me."

Oh no. How could I have been so foolish? "I know you're not, nor do I want you to be. I have Seen so much more than I've ever shown you. When we met, I thought of that vision first because it's my favorite moment with you. We will have fights and tears and dark moments like any other couple, but those are not what I think of first when I look at you. And don't forget how many times you've broken my heart already. But it's all worth going through for all the good I've Seen, for what we shared in the woods. I don't need you to be perfect, just perfect for me."

He wanted to trust her. She wasn't lying, but words were cheap. "Show me."

"What you're asking for—you're not a Seer. Visions can be overwhelming, and five years' worth could be..." She worried her fingers then released them. "...intense, to put it mildly."

He cupped her cheek and looked into her eyes. "I want to know what you know."

"You must be sure. If it's too much for you—if you run..." Her voice cracked. *...you'll break my heart again.*

He brought his other hand to her face. "Give me the chance to share your love. If it's as worthy as you say, I won't go anywhere."

Moira put her hands around his wrists, closed her eyes, and took a deep breath. *My Rhonwin...*

Once again, he saw himself holding her on their wedding night, blissful and enraptured in each other. The scene morphed. Still in his room, he held her, but they wore bedclothes now, and she was crying. He kissed the top of her head and pulled her tight. It changed again, and they were dancing at a festival, bouncing and laughing in rhythm together. Another shift, and she was in his great hall alone, pacing. He entered, and her face lit up. She didn't say a word, but he grinned back and embraced her then placed a hand over her belly. Another change. Moira hugged him, and when she pulled away, she had a visible bulge under her dress. He hiked a bag over his shoulder, then kissed her. She waved as he walked away, and when his back was turned, she wiped her eyes. Another. He put his arm around her shoulder. Hair clung to her damp face and neck. They both looked down at the sleeping newborn in her arms. Another. Rhonwin stomped away and slammed their bedroom door. Moira huffed and slumped onto the bed. Another. She remained on the bed in the same dress, but slightly less light poured through the window. He reentered the room, calm now, and put his hand over hers. She lifted his hand to her cheek then kissed it. He sat down beside her. They curled into each other as the vision faded away.

These are just the beginning. There are more in between them and even more after. She opened her eyes. "Is it too much? Do you need to see more?"

"No, it was enough." He smiled. "It was perfect."

She laughed. "Perfect?"

"Perfect for us, my dear." He leaned in to kiss her.

She put two fingers over his lips. *Where do we stand?* "I need to hear you say it first," she whispered.

He dropped his hands to her waist and drew closer. "I thought I'd acquire the necessary item to do so properly."

Since when has anything about this been proper? "Just say it," she pleaded.

He touched his forehead to hers, and in a low rumble said, "I'm going to marry you."

The words scarcely escaped his lips before she covered them with hers, and he surrendered to her completely.

Rhonwin and Moira will return in the Healers' Kiss series.

THE VEILED QUEEN

a retelling of "King Thrushbeard"

From within the darkest corner of the candlelit hall, Barbenia took a long sip of cider, marveling as the golden son of Boscada reduced another maiden to tears. Barbenia couldn't understand a word of their conversation, but the meaning was clear enough when the offended woman covered her prominent nose and fled the room.

The next woman Prince Elio approached wore a golden tiara—probably a princess—and after they exchanged a few words in yet another foreign tongue, her sturdy frame shook with anger. Not the wisest move. Even at his considerable height, he only had a few inches on her, and she looked more than capable of bashing in his flawless visage.

Without a hint of concern, he turned toward Barbenia. The luster of his fair hair dulled as he stepped into the shadowy nook. He crossed his arms, silently looking her up and down, then cleared his throat.

With the fascinating display of self-destruction, she'd forgotten the advisement to let him hear her speak once before their first conversation. Otherwise, he would continue speaking in the last language he'd heard. She held out her hand. "Good evening, Your Highness. I am Barbenia, Queen of Uskev."

"Hiding from me in the dark?" he asked in perfect Uskevi.

"The view is better from here."

He smirked. "I cannot say the same."

She would not take the bait. "Your palace is lovely."

"Are you sitting back here to hide because of that scar?"

"I am not hiding from anyone," she said coolly.

"You should." He spun on his heels and looked around the room—likely searching for his next target.

Barbenia had not lied. The thin line that ran down the left side of her nose had not bothered her since it healed. Not enough to hide it, anyway. The darkness protected her sensitive eyes, nothing more, but he clearly would not care for the explanation. She had known people like him before, and such reasoning was irrelevant. He would only look for a new scab to pick.

An older version of Elio rushed to her side. "A thousand apologies, Your Majesty," King Lehen said. "Whatever offense he has caused, I shall correct it forthwith."

"I am fine, thank you, but you may want to catch him before he starts a war with a less forgiving queen."

Lehen nodded and in a few long steps, he reached Elio and grabbed his arm. "What do you think you're doing?"

Elio tried to pull away. "Leave me alone."

Strangely, they were not speaking Boscadan. They had both been speaking Uskevi to her and, by a fluke in their shared Gift of Speech, continued speaking it to each other. Unless someone pointed it out, they never could tell what language they were speaking. For all the father and son knew, they were speaking their native language now. If she didn't let on that she could understand them, and nobody interrupted in another language, she could listen indefinitely.

"You can't keep insulting these women. Placating noblewomen is one thing, but the foreign dignitaries?" Lehen shook his head. "For pity's sake, Elio, we'll be lucky if we only lose a few alliances."

"I told you not to press me," Elio said smugly.

"This isn't a game. These decisions affect whole kingdoms."

Elio rolled his eyes. "Why am I part of this? I'm at least sixth in line—no, soon to be eighth. You told me I wouldn't have to concern myself with all this."

Barbenia knew he was the youngest of Lehen's four sons, but not that his brothers were so productive.

"You still have a role to play," Lehen said.

"As a stud for hire to the finest b—"

"Enough! I cannot abide this anymore. If you keep this up, then, by the Giver, I *will* treat you like a dog." Lehen pointed his finger into Elio's chest. "And I expect better than this from one."

Elio scoffed. "You wouldn't dare."

"You're spoiled, Son. I've coddled you for too long. The future you so disdain is one of luxury, and you spit on it. Since you cannot appreciate what you've been given, I will not waste any more resources on you."

He cocked his head back with a sideways glance. "What is that supposed to mean?"

"I'm cutting you off. You will no longer enjoy the easy life of a prince. You can work from now on."

Elio waved him off. "You aren't serious."

"The first employer seeking manual laborers can take you. I expect you to be gone by this time tomorrow." Lehen flagged down a servant and, in Boscadan, began directing him to write something down.

Elio sputtered and let out a stream of angry Boscadan, but Lehen ignored him.

Barbenia finished her drink and walked out onto the terrace. With only the light of the crescent moon, her Night-Sight revealed the palace gardens in stunning clarity, as well as the harbor at the bottom of the bluff. Ornamental trees and grasses filled the garden above, with nary a berry bush or fruit tree in sight. Below, opulent galleons, schooners, and brigs occupied most of the slips. Though Boscada had no shortage of beauty, she hadn't come to see the scenery.

On paper, Elio was the perfect choice for a future consort. Boscada was strong and stable enough to make a valuable ally, but the prince was far enough from the throne to neither be needed here nor threaten the autonomy of her own kingdom. In more capable hands, Speech should have been his greatest asset. And to top it all off, he wasn't bad looking—who was she kidding?—he was gorgeous.

If only his arrogance didn't turn everything to rot.

Barbenia sighed. Would Lehen go through with his threat? He seemed serious enough, but she doubted he could so easily grow a spine after years of caving to Elio. Lehen would change his mind by morning. If Barbenia were in his position, she would've cut Elio off without delay to sooner undo the damage of a lifetime of favoritism.

She had plenty of means to teach him. When she was younger, her father would take her to either the woods or the bay every few months and make her catch dinner for the night. Not born royalty himself, he never let her forget the humbler side of her roots.

She smiled. They were overdue for another outing, and she'd promised to catch a few salmon on the return trip. He wouldn't have to wait long for it. At the rate things were going here, her three-week trip would be over in a few days. Besides the disappointing prince, Lehen's need to put out Elio's fires would distract him from making trade agreements with her.

Ha. Hiring out Elio herself would be a more productive use of her time.

Wait. Could she?

She had the time to spare. If it worked, it'd be worth the effort. And if it didn't...well, she'd appreciate the entertainment.

⚙

Barbenia adjusted her daylight veil as Lehen inspected the deed to her newly acquired ketch.

He frowned. "Such a small vessel. Are you sure this is safe?"

"My men checked its seaworthiness when they purchased it, and I inspected it myself an hour ago. Two guards with Water-Breathing will shadow the boat from below at all times, and we will stay near the archipelago, deep within the Sound and far from open waters." She took back the deed and handed him two contracts. "As I am using my own time and funds for this...venture, I have drawn a trade agreement that I believe you will find fair."

"What about Elio's labor? How does that factor into your equation?"

Barbenia chuckled. "I think we both know what that's worth. Besides, I do not deal in slaves. He will be paid the same as any green deckhand, according to his work. As for the trade agreement, should Prince Elio come to any significant harm in my care, it shall be void."

Lehen raised an eyebrow. "*Significant* harm?"

"This is not a leisurely voyage. I will not void an entire trade agreement if your son gives himself rope burn while manning a sail."

"And this other contract?" He held up the paper. "Who is Thrush?"

"That is my father's surname. The prince will see that contract, and I believe this will work best if he does not know I am a queen."

"But he has met you before."

"Briefly. The veils that guard my vision against the sun will hide my face, and I do not wear a gown to fish. I will be shocked if he makes the connection out of context."

Lehen stroked his chin. "I need to read over these contracts. Meet me here in three hours. Elio will be ready for you then if I agree."

"If? Am I not the first willing employer?" Barbenia put a hand on her hip. "Or are you reneging on your original offer?"

"You expect me to accept this without question?"

Barbenia smiled. "In essence, you wrote it. This is the same proposal you drew up for any royal willing to marrying Elio. I simply replaced any references to marriage with employment."

His eyes widened. "And what will that leave me to offer if he does marry?"

Such a silly, short-sighted question. "He has no marriage prospects now. If you let him continue, his insolence will cost you much more than I am asking for."

He sighed and looked over the contracts again, then turned to one of his servants. "Bring Prince Elio to me."

✻

As if last night's public beratement wasn't enough. What did Father want this time? Elio sauntered into his father's office. "You summoned me?"

"I would like you to meet Captain Thrush." His father gestured to a small woman at his right.

She looked more like a deckhand than a captain. The faded green scarf tied around her hair anchored a gray veil, which shielded her face from the top of her forehead to just past the tip of her nose. Saltwater stains spattered her sun-bleached brown tunic and slops.

"Hello, Captain... Father, why have you called me here?"

"Captain Thrush is your employer now."

Elio laughed. Father had outdone himself this time. Using an actual person to make his point? Elio wasn't a gullible child, easily cowed into submission.

"You have been hired onto her fishing boat."

"Yes, yes, very funny, Father. Was there anything else, or may I go now?"

Captain Thrush held out a stack of rough brown cloth. "You'll need to change into these before we depart."

"I am not putting on those rags."

She shrugged. "If you wanna ruin your fine clothes, suit yourself. You'd best make your goodbyes now."

"Oh, goodbye, Father," he said sarcastically. This farce was becoming annoying.

Father teared up, then turned around and leaned against the window frame, bring a hand to his face. "Have a safe voyage. I will miss you."

Did he think pretending to wipe away a tear would be more convincing?

Thrush clapped a hand to Elio's back. "Come along, greenie."

Elio gasped. He didn't know which was more repulsive: the lack of honorific or the audacity to touch him. "How *dare* you! I am a prince!"

"Not anymore." She brandished a document. "'Cording to this, you're my new deckhand."

He snatched it from her. She was lying. The document couldn't be real. He looked it over and—No, no, no, no no... "You cannot enforce this. I am not willing."

Father crossed his arms. "Your alternatives are to find another employer yourself or take up begging."

Elio's blood ran cold. "Are you banishing me?"

"You will leave with Captain Thrush, or the guards will escort you out," Father said in a tone he reserved for delivering unfavorable edicts. A tone he'd never used with Elio before.

He picked up the ugly clothes. Better to walk out with his head held high than to face the humiliating attention the guards would attract.

Father and Thrush waited outside while he changed. The tunic and slops hung loosely. They might have been comfortable in a proper fabric, but he'd never worn anything in such an atrocious cut. The open air on his calves felt downright strange as if someone had either forgotten to add the last foot of fabric to his pants or stolen the garment from a much shorter and fatter man.

When he exited the office, Father was already gone. Without a word, Elio followed Thrush out of the palace. They wound through the streets, and for the first time, he had to dodge other people; they did not make way for him. The crowds thickened as they walked downhill, suffocating him with their nearness.

Within twenty minutes, they reached the wharf. A pungent low tide punctuated the briny wind. Sailors, dockworkers, and merchants bustled about, shouting over lapping surf and fluttering sails. A sweaty group of workers unloaded fish one by one, using their Ice to freeze them solid with their bare hands. A black and white eagle screamed overhead at a flock of barking gulls. A shining fleet of tall ships, twice as grand as his father's, were moored across a quarter of the docks, all bearing the same blue and yellow banner.

"I wonder whose fleet that is?" Elio said.

Thrush glanced at the ships without breaking stride. "That'd be the Uskevi flag. With a fleet that size, Queen Barbenia herself must be traveling here."

"How do you know about politics?" Such knowledge seemed above a commoner.

"I know boats, and I know the Sound. 'Tween the mainland on both sides and all the islands in the archipelago, different ports usually mean different kingdoms too. Everyone's sailing the same water out there."

As they walked alongside the great ships, their glorious size and sleek paint grew more impressive. "I could have ridden on one of these ships."

"Well, you ain't now. Our boat's just a few yards up ahead here."

She turned down a ramp to a floating dock and stopped in front of the saddest boat in the world. It had only two small masts, the one in front relatively taller than the other. Nets and baskets filled most of the pitiful deck, and several patches dotted the sails.

Elio wrinkled his nose. "*That* is our boat?"

She smiled. "Hop aboard, sailor."

"Where is the rest of the crew? For that matter, where is the rest of the boat?"

She boarded effortlessly. "You *are* the crew."

He crossed his arms. "You lied. You said you were a captain."

"Where's the lie? I've a vessel." She patted a mast. "And I've a crew." She gestured to Elio.

"Of one."

"Still counts." Thrush grinned and held out a hand. "Need help boarding?"

He waved her away and held up his head. "I have boarded a ship before. It is only a foot from the dock."

As he took a large step, the dock shifted backward. He pitched forward into the boat. It tilted downward. He leaned to compensate. His feet slid across the deck until he landed on his rump.

Thrush covered her mouth and snorted.

She thought this was funny? Impudent sea-wench. Elio glared at her. "You moved the boat!"

She held up her hands. "I didn't touch nothing. This ain't as stable as a ship. The dock and the boat move with the water. You'll get used to it."

He didn't want to get used to it.

She fiddled with the sail, tying and untying ropes. "Watch for the boom."

"The what?"

The sail swung around overhead, and the boat strained against the lines holding it to the dock.

She fastened another part. "Work starts now. Throw the lines."

When he didn't move, she pointed back to the dock. "Untie us."

Elio reached for the nearest cleat and began pulling on the knot.

"Ah-ah. Not that one. You'll lose the rope that way. The dock first."

He stretched out to the farther cleat and tugged on the loops. "How was I supposed to know that?"

"Common sense?"

The knot was impossible. No amount of tugging helped. The boat just pulled it tighter again.

With a sigh, Thrush leaned next to him. "Look." She took hold of the rope end that wasn't attached to the boat and yanked the knot free in one motion. As they glided away, she hauled the rope in and coiled it at their feet.

"How did you do that?" Elio asked.

"I'll get there, but let's start with the basics." She pointed to the front of the boat. "That's the bow." She pointed at the back. "That's the stern. We're at starboard, and..."

For half an hour, Thrush taught Elio nautical terms, adjusting the rudder and sails throughout. His head ached from trying to keep up. When she finished zigzagging out of the harbor—or tacking, as she called it—she sat at the stern.

"That wind should be good for a while. You've had a nice little break." She tossed a short length of rope onto his lap and held another aloft. "Now for something more difficult: knot tying."

Elio's fingers throbbed. He couldn't tie another knot.

Thrush frowned at the misshapen mass of rope. "It'll do. I've a more important task for you now anyway."

He leaned his head against the rail and groaned. How could there be more? "Have I not done enough? When is lunch?"

"We need to haul it in first. Up you get."

"You cannot be serious. My hands are ruined!"

She lifted a lid from a large wooden box near the stern. "I let you man the rudder while I set the nets. Consider that your break."

Elio gaped. "That was hours ago." This woman was trying to kill him.

She crossed her arms. "It was only an hour. We're pulling it early so you don't get overwhelmed on your first haul." Steadying the tiller between her knees, she hoisted in a rope over the stern, and a line of wooden buoys moved toward them. "The wind is perfect to gently back us over the net, so

I can help with the net this time. As I bring it in, pull the fish and put them in that box of ice. You'll need to move quickly."

"But—"

"Here they come." She lifted the end of a sheet-like net over the rail, dripping water at their feet. Two-foot salmon hung by their gills at intervals, their heads wedged into the square openings.

He grabbed at one of the fish, but it flopped, and his hands slid over the wet scales. Again he tried, using a firmer grip this time. Its gills ripped and bled. "Ugh!" Elio yelled and dropped the fish. It bounced off the rail into the water with a plop. The same happened with the next two fish.

"Hey! Don't be dropping my catch," Thrush barked.

He shuddered. "They were moving."

She rolled her eyes. "Living things do that. Quit dropping fish overboard, or you'll go with 'em."

Once more, he took hold of a fish. It flopped out of his hands again, but this time, he leaped after it and batted it back before it went over the rail. While the salmon flopped around the deck, he repeated the process until the gillnet was empty.

Thrush turned around. "Get the lid and— Why are there fish roaming my deck?"

"I did not drop them overboard."

She growled. "You incompetent sponge..." She removed a knife from her pocket and flicked it open. "I said to put 'em on ice."

Elio backed against the railing and clutched at it. His feet slid on the wet surface, refusing to flee as he required.

She slashed the knife across the gills of the nearest fish. "All this stress'll ruin their taste. We need to put 'em out of their misery." She handed him another knife. "Cut the gills, and put 'em *on the ice* this time."

He took the knife from her, and they set to work. The first several were easy enough; they were barely wiggling. But many still flopped around. He poked at one with his knife and missed.

"Put the knife down, and grab it with your hands," Thrush said. "One of us is bound to lose a finger if you stab randomly like that. We need to chill the livelier ones to slow 'em down."

They chased the fish across the deck, throwing them on ice and occasionally bumping into one another.

Elio wiped his brow with his sleeve. "This is madness. How do you do this all the time?"

"I don't." She dropped a fish into the box. "The fish ain't supposed to be on deck." She covered the box of ice then sat on it.

He moved to join her but slipped on the briny, bloody deck and landed half on the box with his arm across her shoulder. A slow grin spread below her veil until she cracked up. The melodic noise caught him by surprise, and he found himself laughing with her.

"Oh, Elio." She sighed. "What am I gonna do with you..." She lifted a hand to his face.

He tensed. Was she making an advance on him? The nerve.

"You got fish guts on your cheek." She laughed again as she wiped the offal away.

His face warmed. His dignity was slipping from him like the fish. "We still have a catch, at least."

"This?" Thrush patted the box. "Isn't worth much. It's a small haul, and with the poor handling, only the dogs will eat 'em."

"Surely, we can rest after all that."

She produced an oilcloth bag from behind the box and reached inside. "I'll get lunch ready, but first"—she pressed a bundle of rags into his chest—"you're gonna scrub down this mess. I ain't laying my bedroll in guts."

"Excuse me. Did you just say bedroll?"

✹

Elio squinted and rolled over on the salty bedroll, which did little to cushion him from the wooden planks below. Around him, inky waters melded into spiky profiles, serrating the starscape above. As the boat glided silently through the abyss, only the gentle creak of Thrush's footsteps broke the isolation.

He glanced in the direction of teh sound, but the moonlight was too weak to see by. Thrush might as well have had Invisibility. Nothing but himself and the shadows now. Elio shut his eyes once more.

At home, he'd fought for power over his life. Now he was truly powerless. Perhaps the key was not in fighting.

Perhaps it was in surrender.

✹

Barbenia inhaled the fresh, salty air and gingerly picked her veil off the line where she'd left it to dry overnight. She enjoyed the breeze on her face, but the dawn would soon blind her if she didn't replace her eye cover. Elio didn't concern her. For all his whining that he couldn't sleep on deck last night, exhaustion had faded him in tandem with the sun, and he didn't look close to waking any time soon.

Without the veil or Elio in her way, the night sailing was pleasant. A few stiff winds had let her get some real speed. She would have to manage the sails more today and leave the nets to Elio. Given his ineptitude thus far, she didn't have high hopes for his success.

Barbenia stole one last unfettered look at his sleeping form. The fine layer of stubble and grime did little to mar his looks. If anything, it made him more ruggedly handsome. Ugh. Good thing there were no reflective surfaces on board. That was the last thing his ego needed.

She fastened the veil. It didn't matter how pretty his face was; the man ruined everything he touched. Barbenia reached into her tunic and pulled out a whale pendant, kissing it for luck as Father had taught her, then tucked it back inside.

With her pocket knife and flint, she lit the small pile of cedar chips in her ceramic cooker. When the flame was steady, she laid down pieces of salmon and shielded it with a lid. If the smell didn't wake him, she wouldn't try to. Better that he sleep through cooking. He might set the whole boat ablaze.

Barbenia checked their heading while breakfast cooked. Thanks to the favorable winds overnight, they weren't far from Uskev now. But he wasn't ready for that yet; she was nowhere near finished with him.

Satisfied with the cooking, she suffocated the fire. "Elio," she singsonged, "time to wake." Barbenia dangled a piece of grilled salmon over his nose.

He groaned and rolled over. She poked him in the back with her foot, but he groaned again and swatted at her.

"So much for a pleasant 'good morning.'" Barbenia leaned over the rail and dunked a cupped hand in the frigid water. "Last chance."

Elio didn't stir.

"Suit yourself." She flung the handful of water in his face, flicking her fingers a few times for extra measure.

He gasped sharply and flung himself upward, then sputtered and flailed.

Barbenia smiled. "Gooooood morning, sleepyhead."

"Flaming frog nuggets! I thought I was drowning. You're sadistic."

"Tsk, tsk. Not very princely language."

"I thought I was a sailor now."

She gave a hearty laugh. "True enough." Perhaps she was getting through to him better than she thought. Barbenia offered him a fillet. "Breakfast?"

He wrinkled his nose. "Fish again?"

"I'm sorry, we're all out of roast elk."

He took the proffered food with an apologetic grimace.

Barbenia wolfed down her own breakfast and sat at the stern. "We're coming up on a good spot. Get ready to drop the net."

Elio gulped. "I'm not done eating."

"Hurry up then. If not, you can finish after we drop the gillnet. You'll have more than enough time later."

He shoved the last, large piece in his mouth and joined her at the stern. His cheeks bulged out like a squirrel stuffing nuts.

She covered her smile. Better not to mock him when he'd finally demonstrated a will to work. She cleared her throat. "Feed the net in slowly, starting with this flag. We need the floatline on top and the leadline on the bottom, so don't twist it. And take care over the rail. Lift it over. Don't drag it."

He nodded and picked up the end of the net. To Barbenia's surprise, he followed her directions to the letter. When the sails demanded her attention, she felt secure leaving him to finish on his own.

Elio dropped the last buoy. "Now what?"

She handed him a line. "Let's try your hand at sailing."

Elio tied down the boom and smiled at Thrush. Now that's he'd given up railing against his situation, he found the experience...exhilarating.

Even Thrush was more pleasant. Had she softened toward him, or was it the rush of coastal wind and sea spray making him giddy? Away from the palace, she looked at home on the bow, with her face to the wind. Her rough nautical clothing flowed in the breeze. A midnight braid coiled in and out of her headscarf at her nape. There was a strange, wild beauty to her.

She bounded down the deck. "You're learning well now."

He leaned back on the rail. "I must have a good teacher."

"Now *that* sounds more like someone with Speech. I always thought flattery was second nature to your kind."

"Ha. It's just easier to grasp when you're not worried about translation."

She crossed her arms. "I guess the same goes for insults as well."

He hung his head. "Did my father tell you why he hired me to you?"

"He didn't tell me why you did it. You had every privilege in the world. Why did you throw it away?" Thrush sounded curious, not accusatory.

His father didn't understand. What were the chances that she would? He inhaled and let the breeze wash over him, imbuing him with its freeing exposure.

"I felt trapped," he said. "Growing up, Father sheltered me, showered me with praise. He favored me. When I turned twelve, it only increased his favor."

She nodded. "You got his Gift. Reminded him of himself."

"Exactly. Boscada was prosperous, our neighbors were peaceful, and I was already far from inheriting. I didn't have a care. He ensured that."

"Sounds like you led an easy life."

"It was. When Father heard about the war on the mainland, he changed his mind. Suddenly, it was my responsibility to make an alliance or shore up the loyalty of one of our lords. I was excess personage, too far removed to matter in succession and not trained for anything of consequence."

"He prepared you for nothing and punished you for living up to it," Thrush said matter-of-factly.

Elio gaped. "Yes. I tried to explain it to Father, but he never listened. He only cared when I sabotaged his plans." He had never felt such a sincere connection before, and he fought a peculiar urge to hug her.

She put a hand on his shoulder. "Well, you're not gonna be useless anymore. Fishing's a fine, respectable trade. We're in the Strait of Keesvoy now. You know, a fisherman in these waters once caught the eye of a queen."

He shook his head. "You don't need to make up a legend for my sake."

"No, really. A Baythroan crew was fishing here when an Uskevi fleet passed through. The Uskevi were hungry, and their meat had spoiled unexpectedly early, so they offered to buy the Baythroans' whole haul."

"What about the queen?"

"She was so pleased with her meal, she wanted to thank the fishermen personally. One of 'em made the queen laugh, and she requested to see him again and again and again until, eventually, she made him her consort." Thrush had the smile of someone retelling her favorite story.

The tale sounded so far-fetched to Elio. He'd met an Uskevi queen, and unless she was different from her ancestors, she seemed far too regal to take an interest in the affairs of fishermen. "Do you think it really happened?"

"Every sailor from Baythroas to Uskev will swear to its truth." Thrush looked out over the water. "Ready to circle back to our net?"

"I can try."

She smiled. "Good. You take the sheets. I'll take the tiller."

They tacked back to the net, and Thrush dropped anchor. "The wind is much stronger than before, so I'll need to focus on keeping us steady while you haul. Do you think you can handle it?"

He wanted to get it right this time. "All the fish will be on ice." Elio took hold of the flag buoy. "Ready when you are."

Thrush trimmed the sails again and stood by the tiller. As soon as she weighed anchor, the boat drifted back. Elio heaved the net over the rail, pulling fish out and icing them as quick as he could.

After a few good heaves, his muscles ached. He pulled the net again but failed to lift it high enough, letting it snag on the rail. A palpable ripping sound informed him of his mistake. He panicked, looking for the tear.

"Don't stop." Thrush tugged on a line. "I'm going as slow as I can in this wind. We'll run over the net if you don't pull."

He kept working, taking extra care to lift the net high over the rail, but his strength flagged again and again. By the end of the net, he was ripping it as often as he cleared the rail. He dropped the last fish on the ice and closed the box, then slumped on top of it.

Elio had failed again.

"How's the catch?" Thrush sat down next to him. "I don't see any fish on deck. That's a good sign."

He couldn't look at her. "I—I ruined the net."

"Let's see." She got up and lifted the gillnet, one yard at a time. One- to two-foot holes slashed the netting throughout. She whistled. "That's gonna take a long time to repair...if it's even worth it. We may need a new net."

Disappointing her hurt worse than the blow to his pride. "I'm so sorry. If I knew how, maybe I could do the repair."

Thrush sat next to him. "We can get another net. You're not the first fisherman to destroy one, and you won't be the last. Do you know how many have been lost? They drift away with the current, or the buoys sink, or a whale makes off with it. It happens."

Elio looked at her. "You're not angry?"

"Let me see the haul," she said calmly.

They stood up, and she lifted the lid. Countless salmon filled the box, covering the ice completely.

She grinned and closed the box. "They look to be in good condition. You did well, Elio." She gave him a playful shove. "Not bad for a greenie."

❋

Barbenia pulled the boom tighter and secured the line. The southeaster was perfect for blowing them straight to Uskev. The high speed brought faster winds across the deck than they'd experienced yet. She took the blankets from their bedrolls and approached a shivering Elio at the bow. Wrapping one around him, she said, "You're too cold. Come with me."

He followed her back to the stern, where they sat on the deck in front of the tiller. "What's the plan when we reach port?" he asked.

"We'll offload the haul, buy a new net. We're making good time, but if it's late when we get there, we'll stay overnight." She waited for him to make a fuss about the possibility of a real bed.

He continued shivering under his blanket. "Then I hope we're not late. I don't want you to lose time as well as the net."

Barbenia didn't know what to say. It was the most empathetic thing he'd said since she met him. She moved closer and wrapped her blanket around them both.

Elio looked at her. "It's funny. You've seen me lower than anyone in my life, but I've never seen your face." He slowly brushed his fingers along her jaw, ruffling the edge of the veil as he grazed her ear. His gentle touch called to a deeper craving within her, beckoning her to satisfy it.

Barbenia wrapped her hand around his and lowered it. "It's too bright outside." Though she could have closed her eyes, she wasn't ready to reveal herself yet. She wanted to believe this other Elio was real, but she needed to see what he would do in Uskev.

He laced his fingers between hers. Were his eyes always such an intense pine green? The gray of her veil hardly softened the vibrancy of his gaze, as if he could see right through. He leaned in ever so slightly, his eye line traveling down to her lips, and Barbenia's breath quickened.

"I can wait for starlight," he said.

"Not if you fall asleep first," she teased.

A brief, quizzical frown passed over his face. "Why are you up all day? Surely, you work better at night."

"Who says I don't work at night?"

He leaned back and tilted his head. "But when do you sleep?"

"I rested for an hour after you fell asleep."

"You must be exhausted."

Barbenia shrugged. "I can't let the boat steer itself. We'd run aground in the night."

"Why don't we stay in the harbor tonight, even if it's not late?"

She yawned. "That's tempting."

If the wind kept up, they could sail for an hour without changing tack. Barbenia stretched out her legs and settled back, expecting to feel hard wood against her back. Elio's arm cushioned her instead. She hadn't noticed he was leaning on it.

"Oh, here." He grabbed a bedroll and tucked it behind her.

She smiled. "Thanks." As she sat back, her lids grew heavier. After a few minutes of relative comfort, the weight of her head became too much. She could not deny her body rest for much longer. Like it or not, Barbenia would have to rely on Elio. "Wake me if we...if we..."

"I'll wake you when we're near the harbor."

"But what about...what if..."

Elio chuckled. "Or if we veer off course. You can trust me. Just sleep already."

Her head lolled onto his shoulder. "Don'touchm'veil..." she mumbled.

"I wasn't planning on it."

Sleep overtook her desire to press the issue.

⚓

Elio reached up behind his head and steered a little farther east. Thrush still rested against him, her warmth filling him with contentment. True to his word, he hadn't tried to peek at her face—not that he wasn't tempted.

Ahead, a bright and colorful city perched atop a long wharf. At its peak, a blue and yellow palace spread across half a mile. Lush evergreen forests surrounded it all.

Thrush nestled closer, and Elio smiled. He would have to make larger adjustments soon as they approached the shore, but he hated to wake her. She needed the rest. He laid the second bedroll out on her other side, then gently eased her onto it. Until they made berth, he could continue handling things.

Elio made it to the mouth of the harbor and eased the sails, letting the boat slowly glide toward the docks. Signs pointed the way to docks designated for unloading seafood. He had the boat under control, but it occurred to him that Thrush hadn't taught him how to dock yet.

Dare he try? He'd failed at fishing, but sailing had gone well. He rolled up the mainsail, letting momentum carry them to the pier.

As the boisterous clamor of the wharf overtook them, Thrush bolted upright. "I thought you were gonna wake me."

"I was doing fine," he protested.

She rushed to the bow. "How'd you plan to dock by yourself?"

"The same way I sailed by myself?"

She shook her head. "You can't steer and catch the dock at the same time." Leaning her whole torso over the rail, she reached her arms out and took hold of the edge of the dock, pushing against it and swinging the starboard side toward the pier. "Take the other end."

Elio rushed to his right and followed her movements.

The harbormaster walked over to their section. "What do we have here today?"

"We've a large catch of salmon for Chef Anja," Thrush said.

He wrote in his ledger. "And you are?"

"Thrush."

The man's head snapped up. "Oh, I didn't realize..."

She shook her head slowly. Even for a woman who covered her face, it was an oddly mysterious gesture.

He cleared his throat. "Ah...uh...I'll get some men to unload for you... Have a nice day?" The harbormaster scurried off and flagged down two burly men.

"I'll get the net. You tie up the boat." Thrush said.

Was she going to pretend that was normal? Elio raised an eyebrow. "That was an odd exchange."

She lifted a full armload of netting. "How so?"

"He acted strangely when you told him your name."

"I share a name with a popular captain here." She stepped onto the dock. "Are you coming?"

He quickly looped some rope around the dock and the boat and followed her onshore. The harbormaster watched as they passed, but he turned away when he realized Elio was watching back.

There was something weird about that man.

Not far down the wharf, Thrush led Elio to a net-maker. The little old man looked over the damage. "I could repair it," he said, "but the time'll cost you more than a new one. I could buy this one off you for scrap and—"

Someone shouted. A crowd formed on the pier they'd just left. Elio and Thrush ran to see the cause of the commotion.

Two dockworkers held the box from Thrush's boat aloft, and the dock beside them was empty.

The boat was drifting into the harbor.

Frog nuggets. Was there nothing he couldn't foul up?

Elio took off toward it. He couldn't let her boat get away.

Thrush jumped in front of him, arms outstretched. "What do you think you're doing?"

He reached for the hem of his shirt. He'd want it dry when he got out of the water. "This is my fault. I'm going to get it back."

She pressed him back. "No, you're not. That water is deep and, more importantly, cold. You can't swim in that."

"But—"

"*No!*" She took his face him both hands, forcing him to look at her. "That boat's not worth drowning for. Either another boat'll catch it, or high tide'll wash it back."

He dug his hands into his hair. "I lost the boat."

"I know."

"I lost the boat." He couldn't fail any harder than that. The fish. The net. They were nothing compared to the entire boat.

What was worse: he'd lost *her* boat.

She took his hands. "Just breathe, Elio. Come with me." She led him a bench, far from the crowd, and sat him down. "I know you already feel terrible, but I'm afraid I'm going to have to end our contract," she said gently, putting a hand on his shoulder. "Without a vessel, I don't have any work for you."

He went numb. "I have nowhere to go," he murmured.

She reached into her tunic and pulled a thin gold necklace over her head. "Take this." She pressed the pendant into his palm. Time and hands had worn the white jade orca smooth. "My father works in the palace. Go there, and ask for Thrush. Show them this pendant. He will help you."

More strangeness from his mysterious captain—or former captain—but he had no right to demand answers now. "You won't come with me?"

"I have my own matters to deal with."

Elio put the necklace on. "Will I ever see you again?"

She nodded. "I'm sure of it. Just promise me you'll go to the palace and ask for Thrush."

"I promise." After all he'd done, he couldn't believe she was helping him. He would have promised anything to thank her. He would make this right someday...somehow.

"Until we meet again, Elio." Thrush walked away without looking back.

It took all of Elio's willpower not to chase after her.

As Barbenia stepped into the welcome dimness of her private wing, she peeled away her veil and scarf. "I brought your favorite dinner with me," she said in Baythroan.

Father's face lit up as he hugged her. "You're back awfully early."

She shrugged wearily. "Plans changed."

"Should I be worried?"

"Not at all. Lehen signed the best possible agreement. Uskev got everything it needed." Despite the overwhelming political success, a sense incompleteness nagged at her.

He cast a wary glance over her shoulder. "If that's the case, why are you alone? I thought he'd only sign that in exchange for a marriage."

"We struck a bargain. There's no marriage," she admitted.

He grinned.

Barbenia put a hand on her hip. "Why are you smiling?"

"I'm sorry. You know how I feel about those kinds of arrangements." He'd always reminded her that she never would've been born had her mother married for politics. He wanted Barbenia to find love as they had.

She sighed. "Yeah, well, you might be right. I may have...I don't know." Elio was attractive, and she'd felt *something* between them, but she couldn't dare to speak her emotions into being. What if she were wrong?

Father's smile turned bittersweet. "You look so much like your mother just now."

Barbenia squeezed his hand, blinking back the threat of tears. She cleared her throat. "I have a favor to ask—well, a few, actually."

Pausing to catch his breath, Elio ran his thumb over the whale pendant and looked around the courtyard. It'd taken at least a dozen wrong turns to get this far, but he'd finally made it to the palace. Though many winding paths had led upward, it was difficult to judge where they'd end from downhill.

He caught the attention of a helpful guard, who directed him to the servants' entrance. There, another guard with Speed zipped in front of him as Elio attempted to step inside.

"I don't recognize you, and you're not delivering anything. State your business," the guard said.

"I'm here to see a man named Thrush. Someone told me he works here."

"I'll let him know you're here to see him. And you are?"

"He wouldn't know me." Elio removed the necklace and held it out. "I was told to show him this."

"Wait here." The guard ducked in and whispered something to a servant before turning back to Elio. "He should be out shortly. You can have a seat for now." The guard gestured to a wooden stool a few feet out of the way outside.

Elio sat with his back against the yellow siding. Before long, a simply dressed man with black hair walked out. As he approached, the fine quality of his plain attire became more apparent. He had to hold a respected position here.

The man stopped in front of Elio. "You asked to see me?"

Elio lifted the pendant. "My name is Elio." His title was irrelevant now. "Your daughter sent me. She said you could help."

"With?"

"She hired me onto her boat, but I'm afraid I bungled everything..." He recounted their whole voyage—omitting the part about snuggling under a shared blanket, of course. "...and I have nowhere else to go."

"I see," the elder Thrush said. "Come with me."

Elio followed him inside. The first corridor was the same painted wood as the outside, but the interior grew more grand and detailed as they ventured deeper in, far past where a man dressed in fishy rags should be allowed to wander. They walked for ages until they reached a dimly lit passage.

Thrush's father knocked and entered a room. "Wait here."

It seemed everyone was saying that. Elio couldn't remember waiting for anyone in his life until today, but change itself had developed into a pattern lately—as had failure. Only one of those things was worth fighting.

He rocked on his heels and took in his surroundings. Even in the soft candlelight, he could make out the fine wooden inlay of the panels on the wall. His father would envy such a beautiful palace.

What kingdom was he in? He'd never thought to ask, and it seemed a silly question now. His inability to distinguish what language people spoke did not help. He should've paid more attention to the flags he'd passed along the way.

The door opened, and Thrush's father beckoned him closer. "Her Majesty has graciously agreed to an audience and is, fortunately, free to meet right now."

Elio gaped. "Her Majesty?" Who would have guessed Thrush was so well connected? Elio wished he'd thanked her more profusely for such a favor.

"The Queen of Uskev is a busy woman. Best not to keep her waiting."

Elio stepped forward stiffly. Uskev? That would be Queen Barbenia. His breath caught in his throat. Oh no. He hadn't been kind to her in the brief time they met. She would be justified to throw him out on sight. But he needed to atone for all his mistakes, not just the ones against Thrush. He took a deep breath to steady his knees and pressed himself into the shadowy room.

Sumptuous jewel-toned fabrics draped around the room. Queen Barbenia occupied a rich blue armchair at the center. A red satin gown flowed over her. Raven hair fell in tousled waves around an elegant face. The hairline scar he'd disparaged before was of little consequence to her striking appearance.

Elio bowed low. "Thank you for your time, Your Majesty."

She regarded him coolly. "I have been informed of your plight. What skills do you have?"

"I have Speech and recently learned to fish and sail, though my proficiency in both is severely lacking."

"I currently have little use for an interpreter."

Elio clasped his hands together. "Please, Your Majesty. I will do whatever you ask, but I must work. My request is not for my own sake, but for the woman whose boat I lost."

Her expression softened. "You ask nothing for yourself?" Her tone was so familiar.

He lowered his head. "I have not earned it."

"On the contrary. You did well, Elio. Not bad for a greenie."

Impossible. He looked up gradually. Her mouth. He knew that mouth. He'd caressed that jaw, wanted to kiss those lips.

Elio turned to Thrush's father. He had the exact same shade of dark hair as his daughter—and the queen.

Elio blinked. It wasn't real. A dull ache lodged in his chest. She wasn't real...

"I apologize for hiding my title," Barbenia said, "but I promise everything else was true. Speaking of which, I don't think the two of you have been properly introduced. This is my father, Hector Thrush."

Hector held out his hand. "Pleased to meet you, Elio."

Elio shook it cautiously. "The fisherman who married a queen?"

"They call me Prince Hector or the Prince Father now, but yes."

Elio turned back to Barbenia. "This was revenge for how I treated you, wasn't it?" Giver knew he deserved it, but it didn't fit with the woman he'd come to know.

"No, not revenge," she said softly. "I did not wish to strike you down. I gave you a chance to grow, to become a better man."

True. She could have been much crueler if revenge were her aim. "Why the ruse?"

"If I came to you as a queen, my orders would have been a show of power. So I humbled myself by your side."

"And my father?"

She took a deep breath. "He signed a trade agreement in return for this arrangement, but my end of the bargain is fulfilled. You are free to do as you please now."

"What do you mean 'free'?" His father had used that word too many times in reference to his so-called choice of marriage.

"If you want to return home, I will order a ship at once. If you wish to stay in Uskev, you may stay. My father has generously offered to teach you more fishing and sailing if that's what you desire."

Hector stepped forward. "We can have a boat ready by tomorrow."

"If you want something else instead, simply ask," Barbenia said.

"Anything?"

She smiled. "Within reason. If you wanted to take up pickpocketing, I couldn't help you."

Elio knew what he wanted. The desire had been with him before he stepped foot in the palace. He'd thought his chance had sailed away with the boat, but here it was again.

"I now realize that even as a prince, I did not deserve to ask, but I come to you, even less deserving now as the worst fisherman in the world,"—Elio dropped to his knees and bowed his head—"and humbly request your hand."

The silence was interminable. He had overstepped his bounds. Her gown swished quietly. Why didn't she answer?

A red satin hem appeared at his knees. Barbenia knelt down and took both of his hands in hers. Elio lifted his head.

She smiled as tears trailed down her beautiful face. "I would love nothing more."

Barbenia and Elio will return in the Healers' Kiss series.

GIFTS

Allure – naturally more likeable, possibly seductive; can lead to paranoia
    from overuse

Animal Speech – can speak to animals; socialize better with them than
    people; trouble with impulse control

Far-Sight – telescopic vsion; terrible near vision

Fire – can expel heat from body

Flight – can fly; large wings can be unwieldy on the ground

Healing – can heal others; compromised self-healing and immune system

Hearing – extremely sensitive ears

Ice – can absorb heat into body

Invisibility – cannot be seen by others

Listening – always reads everyone's thoughts

Memory – can never forget anything

Near-Sight – microscopic vision; terrible far vision

Night-Sight – enhances light for constant nocturnal vision; daylight painful

Seeing – receives visions of the future; no control over visions

Speech – can speak any language; cannot identify languages

Speed – can move at incredible speed; eats four times as much

Stone-Skin – skin is armored; also lacks emotional sensitivity

Strength – has the strength of four men; eats as much as two men

Transformation – can turn into a known mammal; can go insane from
    overuse

Water-Breathing – can breathe underwater; cannot leave water for more
    than a day

ABOUT THE AUTHOR

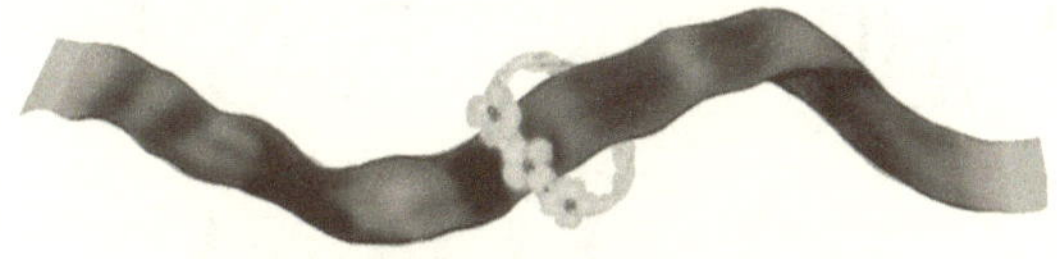

Brandi Spencer's love stories of Carum Sound are heavily influenced by the beautiful Pacific Northwest, where she lives with her husband and two sons. The scenic views of Puget Sound and the Cascades provide plenty of inspiration for her superpowered fantasy romances. A Western Washington University alumna and former cosmetologist turned work-at-home mom and homeschool teacher, she writes in between family life and work for A4A Publishing. She loves crafting, baking, and video games and spends far too much time researching for her stories.

Follow her online:

www.BrandiSpencer.com
Twitter: @Meriverian
Facebook: @Meriveran
Instagram: @Meriverian

ALSO BY BRANDI SPENCER

HEALERS' KISS I

KISS OF TREASON

Two forbidden lovers share the rare gift to heal others with a kiss—but at a cost.

Amid culture clashes and threats of war, Odelia and Kennard navigate a world where power always has a price. If they choose the wrong paths, they could destroy not only their hearts but lives and nations.

And a kiss might not be strong enough to save them...

books2read.com/kisstreason

Authors 4 Authors Publishing

A publishing company for authors, run by authors, blending the best of traditional and independent publishing

We specialize in speculative fiction: science fiction, fantasy, paranormal, and romance. Get lost in another world!

Check out our collection at https://books2read.com/rl/a4a
or visit Authors4AuthorsPublishing.com/books

For updates, scan the QR code or visit our website to join our semi-monthly newsletter!

Want more fantasy romance? We recommend:

FYR

by Lisa Borne Graves

At seventeen, Toury arrives in Fyr, where magic is power, a prince's love is deadly, and female autonomy is a dream. Alex, the Prince of Fyr, has to face his father's ailing health, the expectation to marry soon, and the hidden necromancers trying to take over the realm by exploiting his dark curse. At least there's hope in a cheeky savior, but Earth girls aren't so easy. Can they trust each other enough to save Fyr? Or will everything they hold dear turn to ash?

books2read.com/fyr